THE SECRET

KEVIN LYNCH

INKUBATOR
BOOKS

Published by Inkubator Books
www.inkubatorbooks.com

ISBN (eBook): 978-1-915275-83-7
ISBN (Paperback): 978-1-915275-84-4
ISBN (Hardback): 978-1-915275-85-1

PROLOGUE

I saw the knife, and everything around me stopped for a moment. Even the birds seemed to go silent. There was no movement, nothing for me to focus on but the knife. Its long, black wooden handle and then the blade, gleaming with a sickening sparkle in the bright afternoon sunlight. The bottom of the blade was wide, but it quickly tapered into a fine point, sharp and deadly, and it was close to me, so close that if I dared to move, it would be in me in seconds. Its cold, deadly steel would pierce me, cutting through everything that was keeping me alive.

I was stuck, rigid, unable to react. The fear was all-encompassing, like nothing I had ever felt before.

Time had stopped.

The person holding the knife was looking at me, and their eyes were cold and hard, flashing with hatred for me. Nothing had prepared me for this moment. This person... how could they do this? Was there anything I could say or do to stop them?

Even as I scrambled desperately for words, I knew my

throat was too dry, too constricted to speak them. The words would most likely come out as feeble, whispered sounds.

I knew I couldn't scream either. Nobody would hear my breathless sounds before the knife would slice into me, spilling my blood, draining my life away.

I tried to think of something I could do to stop it, but the blade was too close. I didn't dare budge or make any movement that would cause the person in front of me to act, to end my life. All I could do was pray that someone would intervene, something would stop this.

If not, these would be the last moments of my life.

1

NICOLE

I had met Alan at reception, where I usually met all new clients, and he'd immediately struck me as different. As a counsellor, I was used to people looking either timid or frightened, or sometimes overly confident in a brash kind of way, but he had been none of these. He had been tall, athletic looking with olive skin and thick, brown, wavy hair, which he'd parted to one side that day. His file said he was thirty-one, although he could have passed for younger. The overall impression I had gotten was of someone who was deeply comfortable in their own skin.

He walked with an easy gait as I led him to my therapy room.

My room was wide and high-ceilinged, and one of a number of counselling rooms that were located in this three-storey Georgian building a couple of miles from the centre of Dublin. My office was on the ground floor, and I shared the space with half a dozen other counsellors.

Alan sat in one of the two soft-cushioned chairs that I had arranged on either side of a low, smoked-glass coffee table. There was a box of tissues on the client's side of the table and

a couple of incense sticks in the centre. The room was deliberately sparse apart from some prints of impressionist paint-
ings that I used to give the décor a bit of a lift. I also had an
old, wooden clock on the mantelpiece, which I used to keep
time on my sessions.

'Nice place,' he said as he sat, throwing an appraising eye
around the room.

'Thanks. It's roomy. Can be a bit cold in the winter
though.'

He nodded at a blocked-up space where the fireplace
used to be. 'Must have taken a fair few buckets of coal to keep
this place warm back in the day.'

I sat, took out my notebook and went through the T's and
C's of counselling: commitment, time, boundaries, confidentiality and cost. He nodded as I read them out, like we were
business associates agreeing to the finer points of a deal. That
was fine by me. Clients were often surprised by the initial
formality of the interaction, but not Alan. He took it in his
stride.

With that out of the way, I turned to him and asked
directly, as I always do, 'So what brings you here?'

This time I saw him flinch, a little tic that flashed across
one eye and disappeared just as quick. He adjusted in his seat
and ran his hands down his legs; then he laughed. I was
familiar with nervous laughs and sympathised, but I didn't
feed into it, so I kept a neutral expression and said nothing.

'It's kind of hard to say,' Alan said.

'Is there any one particular thing that's troubling you?'

'I guess there is, but it's a long story.'

'Well, we have plenty of time, so you can start wherever
you like.'

Alan combed his fingers through his hair. I saw that little
tic flash across his eye again. He smiled, but it was a forced
smile. His teeth were gritted.

'You mightn't think it to look at me, but I had a rough upbringing. I don't even know if you would call it an upbringing. Dragged up by the scruff of the neck would be more like it.'

He laughed, and I got the impression it was a line that he'd had to use more than once. There was a charm there but also vulnerability. He had packaged himself really well, and he was right, I mightn't have immediately thought rough upbringing, but one thing I had learned as a therapist was not to make assumptions about anyone who walked through the door.

'The thing is,' he continued, 'it's all had an effect on me. I manage. I manage really well, in fact – good job and all that – but I have this temper, and I don't know where it comes from.'

'Do you notice anything in particular that triggers your temper?'

He shifted uneasily in the chair again and switched his gaze to the door – again a common enough reflex for clients who were struggling. During sessions, the door suddenly took on a magical appeal. The pain of articulating what they were going through was sometimes too much for the client. Running for the door was always an attractive option.

'It's... I suppose, mostly in relationships – well, I'm not sure you would actually call them relationships because they never last that long.' He stopped there and looked at the floor.

'Okay, maybe you should tell me a bit more about your background so I get a better picture of where you're coming from.'

That led to another short silence. Then Alan took a deep breath and started.

'My memories of home are just shouting and trouble. Both my parents drank, and there was never money in the house. I was the youngest of three. I don't have much contact with my siblings. They both legged it to Australia as soon as they could legally board a plane on their own.' He smiled wistfully at the thought of them. 'Don't get me wrong though, we stay in touch through Facebook. Just... they've got their lives over there and nothing here, so why would they come back?

'I was running wild from age twelve, and my parents were too far gone then, so I was taken into care – couple of foster homes, then a residential unit. I met all sorts in the unit and got into everything the city had to offer someone who was out of control.'

He took another pause, but I could see he was getting into the rhythm of talking and had accepted that he needed to begin the process of opening up.

He ran his fingers through his wavy, brown hair and looked off to the side. 'Running wild like that leads to the law courts, and I spent plenty of time there – short remands, probation services, all of that. I never did time – not a long stretch anyway, always got off by the skin of my teeth.' He smiled again. 'Lucky me, eh?'

I said nothing. I didn't want to interrupt his flow.

He started again after a short break. 'Guess I did get lucky once I left the care home and went into semi-independent living. My key worker really stood by me and landed me an opportunity in retail – high-end clothes. I had always been into my clothes, so I was able to blag my way through an interview. They gave me a chance, I think, because my key worker just kept pushing. And that's where I am today, in a management role, plenty of money – what looks like success to most people, but it doesn't feel that way to me. Like I said, I've got this anger, and it just flares up out of nowhere. I keep driving people away. Can't say I blame them. Who'd want to stick with a headcase like me?'

'And what was life like with your parents when you were there?'

'Chaotic, like I said. I missed more school than I went to. My da was the heavier drinker, but my ma put in a good shift herself. I had to get myself up most mornings, but that didn't go too well. Then we had the school on to us about my lack of attendance, then the Educational and Welfare Board. I got a lot of the blame for that. Got a couple of wallops from the da for my troubles. We weren't exactly the Brady Bunch.'

'Did you have friends then?'

'No, not really. Couple of other headcases in the school would go off smoking or drinking or whatever. But then my parents lost the house we were in, and we had to move way out of the city, and that put an end to the headcases. I spent a lot of time on my own, just going into town, hanging around amusement arcades – that sort of thing.'

Alan gave me a little more background, and then we finished our session. He looked both shaken and relieved at the same time. It had probably been a long time since he'd opened up like that – if at all. All colour had drained from his youthful face. Yet he loped with as much confidence as he could towards the door and smiled back at me as he left. I had given him some relaxation and mindfulness tips to help if he felt any sudden anxiety coming on.

I had a couple more clients that morning, and after lunch, then, as I did a couple of times a week, I met with Dorothy, the centre manager and our counselling supervisor. All counsellors regularly discussed new clients with her and flagged anything that we felt might cause us difficulty as counsellors, or if we felt overwhelmed by what we'd heard in a session.

Her office was to the right of the upstairs front door as you came into the building. I knocked before going into her room, which she always managed to keep tidy and ordered despite the volume of clients and accompanying issues that came through our doors.

She was typing something as I walked in, and nodded to a seat off to one side. Dorothy was still remarkably young looking, with shoulder-length blonde hair and sparkling, gold-rimmed glasses. She had small, neat features in a face that dared you to look for flaws in her smooth skin. I knew Dorothy was pushing fifty, if not more, but she had the energy and vitality of someone much younger.

'Now, Nicole,' she said as she swivelled round to face me, 'sorry about that. Just had to get that email off my to-do list.'

I imagined Dorothy's to-do list was extensive, but I also imagined she would have no problem ploughing efficiently through it.

I shuffled through my files and gave her a brief summary of my clients, new and old, but I gave special attention to Alan, because he was new and because he was a little out of the ordinary. Dorothy listened and nodded as I went briefly through his profile without giving any personal data away. We kept client information confidential unless we thought the client was at risk. Dorothy zeroed in on the fact he had been in a care home for so long and also the latent aggression that he reported.

'What I am thinking, Nicole, is that this reminds me of that previous case with Gary Mulligan.'

I had hoped she wouldn't bring that case into the frame, but it didn't surprise me that she had. Gary Mulligan had been a difficult client who'd developed an infatuation with me that had led to him stalking me and my ex-partner Daniel.

'I know there are similarities, but I can't spend my professional life avoiding younger male clients just because of what happened. I thought we had spoken about that before.'

'We had. But it doesn't mean you shouldn't still be careful.'

'*Aware*, I think was what we had said after Mulligan. I needed to be aware.'

Dorothy fixed me with a stare. 'You were traumatised by that, Nicole. Trauma has a way of twisting itself into so many aspects of our being. We aren't aware of where it hides and in what form it can manifest.'

'I think I am aware. I've studied the effects of trauma.' I probably sounded irritated when I said that because Dorothy looked sharply at me over her gold-rimmed spectacles.

'I know you have studied trauma, Nicole. We all have, and we have experienced it in all its forms during therapy sessions, but it doesn't mean we are aware of our own trauma. That's why we have supervision, to make sure we are not being triggered, or of countertransference.'

I didn't know what to say to that. Dorothy was right. Trauma can make us act in ways that are outside of our own awareness. Would my own trauma influence the way I interacted with Alan? I had to listen to her counsel, but I was determined not to let it affect my sessions with him.

There was something about him that was different, something intriguing, and I was determined to help him work through it. But Dorothy was right. Trauma did affect us in different ways and leave parts of us hidden until we got triggered and acted out in ways we might never have thought possible.

I know, because I was one of those people.

2

DANIEL

The shop was quiet. It had been quiet for the past couple of days. Weekends were busy, and that was what kept the place afloat, but on weekdays there was this ominous lag. People didn't want to buy high-end handcrafted gifts and souvenirs during the week. But my suppliers still wanted payment for their stock – thirty days credit was the norm. The bills and the rent kept coming; the rates kept rising. There were days when I just let the invoices pile up because I couldn't face looking at another final demand.

I walked around the shop and fixed a couple of items so they looked more presentable, all the while hoping to catch the eye of a passing group of tourists who might jump at the chance to buy a handcrafted piece of jewelry or a nicely sculpted chunk of bog oak. I had faith in the goods and felt it was only a matter of time before things really took off. Dublin was awash with tourists. It was just a question of word getting around, and they would be flooding in.

The situation with Nicole's past client, Gary Mulligan, hadn't helped, but that was only a minor setback. It had

scared the crap out of me and the few customers who had
been in the shop at the time, but I hoped that was now buried
firmly in the past.

Nicole had gone back to counselling practice after a short
break. She had to. It was her livelihood. But the worry stayed
with me. *What if the same thing happens again?* Clients became
infatuated with their therapists. Nicole was attractive, in her
late thirties. The fact that it could easily happen weighed on
my mind.

That had been the nail in the coffin for our relationship.
We had been on rocky territory before that, partly because of
my decision to quit a steady job in teaching so I could open a
shop. It had put us under financial pressure, and we'd argued
a lot about who was going to be at the school gate for our ten-
year-old son, Ben. Now parenthood was even more compli-
cated because we lived apart, and both of us had started new
relationships – me with Pamela and her with her Spanish
teacher, Pablo. Our son had become volatile in school, and I
felt the stress of his parents splitting was taking its toll
on him.

Pamela had been collecting him from school, and I
wondered how Ben felt about that. We had decided to be
straight with him about the whole thing and explain that
these things sometimes happened, and relationships
changed, and it had nothing to do with him. Ben was usually
a quiet kid who kept his thoughts to himself, so he hadn't said
that much to me about it.

I shut up shop after selling just one hand-carved, wall-
mounted wooden clock and an aquamarine birthstone
pendant. I jumped in my car and drove home, picking up a
banana smoothie on the way as a treat for Ben.

'Hi, love,' Pamela greeted me with a kiss inside the door of
our apartment.

I could see Ben's head of curly brown hair as he sat in the

background, playing a computer game. I worried about how much time he was spending gaming, but I said nothing about it. I would talk to him about it when the time was right. I went straight over to him and rubbed his shoulders.

'How's the little man. Are we winning?'

He shrugged his shoulders to release my grip. I was probably breaking his concentration. I took a shower, and we sat around our small wooden table for a dinner of shepherd's pie and side salad.

'How are the scholars?' I asked Pamela and Ben, flicking my eyes mischievously from one to the other.

'Scholars?' Ben asked with a frown.

'Someone who studies,' Pamela explained.

Ben stared at a piece of pie he had speared with his fork and gave a slight nod.

'I study human resources,' Pamela said.

'You study what?' Ben's frown deepened.

'Human resources, someone who makes sure people are happy in their jobs,' Pamela continued.

Ben went wordlessly back to his pie.

'Pamela is trying to get a better job,' I added. 'Sometimes you have to study more to do that.'

Pamela had been doing clerical work in a gas company for years, and she wanted a meatier role. It would mean more money as well, as her current role only paid her a basic wage.

I turned to my son. 'What about you, little man?'

'What about me?'

'Homework?'

'Finished.'

'Oh, that was quick.' I glanced at Pamela for confirmation.

'I didn't see Ben do it, but maybe he had very little.' Pamela and I had discussed our parenting approach with Ben and had decided to take a softly-softly approach until he warmed to the new set-up. The split with Nicole had been sudden, and I had met Pamela soon after. She was a few years younger, in her early thirties, and it would probably take time for him to accept her.

Ben looked up at Pamela. 'You're very old to be studying.'

Pamela put her fork on her plate. I could see the blood rising in her face. 'I am not old, and that is a very rude thing to say,' she said with a clipped tone.

'People can study at any age,' I said quickly.

'I haven't seen anyone her age studying,' Ben said. He put venom into his emphasis of 'her'. Pamela glared at him. I quickly rested my hand on hers to calm her rising temper.

'Pamela made the decision to go back and study, but it wasn't easy. She wants to do more with her life, and I think that is something to be admired.'

'Maybe, but she shouldn't be saying anything to me about my homework. She's not my mother.'

'Yes, but she wants to look after you and make sure you are doing the best for yourself.' I could hear the strain in my own voice and felt Pamela trying to pull her hand away from mine.

Ben pushed his chair back and stomped off to his bedroom. I was tempted to go after him but held back, deciding that it was better to leave him to cool off. I squeezed Pamela's hand, and she pulled away from me.

'He can't talk to me like that. I won't put up with it.'

'He'll settle down. Don't worry. It's just all the upheaval is a lot for him to take in.'

'You've been saying that for weeks. When is he going to "settle down" as you call it?'

I took a deep breath and looked at Pamela. She was an attractive woman with straight, dark hair that she had tied back in a ponytail. She wore little makeup, and that allowed her fresh, peachy complexion to shine through. Pamela looked after herself with lots of yoga at home and classes twice a week.

I had met her in a local café after one such session, when she had forgotten her wallet but had already ordered a coffee. I paid for her coffee, and we just got talking, and things had flowed very naturally from there. Friends told me I had rushed into the whole thing, and it was too soon after Nicole to have someone move in, but it had felt right at the time.

I reached out for her hand and held it again on the table. 'We'll work through this together. Ben will eventually come around, but we can't force it. We have to move at his pace. There have been huge changes in his life, and we have to accept that's just going to be difficult for him.'

Pamela didn't say anything. At least it was an improvement on the anger I had seen building earlier. This wasn't going to be easy. I just hoped that Nicole, now back in practice, had learned from the previous incident and that at least part of our lives could return to a semblance of normality.

3

NICOLE

I welcomed the distraction of Spanish class on Thursday evening. I had done a little Spanish in school, and my grasp of the language was quite basic. Still, it gave me the opportunity to stare up at the new love of my life, Pablo. He was medium height with dark-brown hair and an expressive face, thanks to those deep-brown eyes that had mesmerized me from the get-go. I wouldn't have placed him as typically Spanish-looking, but I did understand enough about Spanish culture to know that there were lots of variations on the Iberian theme.

Pablo moved his thin body around the class quickly, but he spoke quite slowly – a contrast that I found intriguing. During class, I did my best not to smile up at him too much, as I knew he found it distracting, and we weren't sure how many of the students had put two and two together. During the break – it was a two-hour class – I left him to circulate among the students, but after class, as far as I was concerned, he was all mine.

That evening, after class, I waited for him outside the language school, and as it was a mild late-spring evening, we were happy to dawdle as we made our way back to my place. Pablo lived in the city centre, sharing an apartment with friends. Going back to my house, with its front and back gardens, complete with a lush, weeping willow tree, was a nice break from the relentless concrete landscape of the city.

'You getting used to the past tense yet?' Pablo asked with a smile.

'I haven't got used to the present, never mind the past. Unless of course we're talking about this present now, because I find that very easy to get used to.' We were holding hands, and I gave his a squeeze for emphasis so he'd be clear I was talking about us with a capital *U*.

He paused to light a rolled cigarette. Pablo only smoked a little, but when he did, he sucked hungrily at the thinly rolled cigarettes like they were going out of fashion. He had the courtesy not to smoke in the house, not even after we made love, and I appreciated that. I was struggling with stopping smoking myself. The incident with the stalker had me reaching too often for the comfort of a cigarette. I was only smoking a few a day, but I wanted to knock the habit on the head.

'Yeah, is nice walking with you too, darling.' He gave me a quick tobacco-scented kiss on the cheek. Pablo had excellent English, but one thing he couldn't seem to get his head around was saying *it's*, so he truncated it to *is*.

'How quaint. Not many people use the word darling anymore, you know.'

'Quaint?' He wrinkled his nose, as if his lack of under-standing of the word had caused him actual pain.

'Cute, in an old-fashioned way.'

'Oh, nice.'

'Yeah, nice, like you. Funny, isn't it, how I just walked into the right Spanish class three months ago, and wham, off we went.'

'Maybe someone watching over you.'

'Maybe. About time too after what I went through with the stalker guy.'

'Nasty business, yeah. He's lucky I wasn't around for that.'

'Now, now. That's not the answer to anything. He was a client, you know. Hazards of the job.'

'Yeah, but to pick on a woman. Nasty.'

I was charmed by the protective, macho stance Pablo was taking, but at the same time was glad he hadn't been around. The stalker – Gary – had got lost in a world of trans-ference where he saw me as some sort of idealized love object. It had been really scary at the time, but a head-on confrontation would have made things a whole lot worse. The police had got involved, and that had been the best way to resolve it.

'Shall we walk a little faster?' I said after a bit. 'Daniel is dropping Ben over, and maybe we could get a bit of quality time in before he comes?'

'Okay. Now you're talking,' Pablo said with a laugh. He liked using popular expressions like 'now you're talking' and was pretty adept at slotting them in the right place.

We rounded the corner to the quiet street where my two-storey red-brick was nestled in among some pine trees. It was a quiet estate that curved around in a boomerang shape and ended in a cul-de-sac. James, my next-door neighbour, was pulling into his drive as we turned to walk into mine. He gave me a cursory wave and a smile as he unstrapped his three-year-old from a car seat in the back.

'Hi, James,' I shouted over, but kept going towards my front door, as time was short. Ben would be over within the hour.

'Race you upstairs,' Pablo said as we shut the door. Like a couple of teenagers, we ran upstairs and into the master bedroom, where we threw ourselves on the bed, and I let the lithe, muscular feel of his body pressed against mine take me to a warm, satisfying place.

I heard the doorbell ring as I was stepping out of the shower and trotted down the stairs in my dressing gown. I opened the door and gave Ben a quick hug as he dashed through the door. Daniel idled on the porch. It still felt strange to have the man I had shared my life with for so many years stand awkwardly on the porch of his old house, but we were getting used to our separate lives slowly but surely.

'Everything okay?' I asked Daniel.

'Yeah, Ben's probably a bit tired, but the homework's done, anyway.'

I wondered if there was a little dig there at me over coming back late from Spanish class, but it was something I really enjoyed, so no way was I conceding ground on that.

'Don't worry. I'll sort him out and get him to bed. How's Pamela?'

'Good, studying away.' Daniel nodded, as if to reinforce his answer. I was glad he had met somebody else so quickly. I had my reservations about Pamela, but I kept them to myself. She seemed a bit grabby or something, but I knew I had to give her time. She would probably prove me completely wrong.

'How's Pablo?' Daniel asked.

I almost laughed. It was like we were exchanging formal courtesies.

'Yeah, he's well. Looking forward to seeing Ben.'

Daniel nodded. 'I think Ben has a couple of new Spanish words to practice. He's mad for the Duolingo.'

'He's coming on. Got a bit of an aptitude for languages does our Ben.'

Daniel laughed at that, then shook his car keys in a gesture that indicated he was ready to depart. Unconsciously, I twisted the engagement ring that Daniel had got me. It was on my middle finger now that we were divorced. I liked the ring – platinum, with an opal in the centre – so I kept it. Besides, Daniel and I still got along. For me, the ring was a reminder of the good times we'd had together.

'Okay, see you day after tomorrow,' I said. I was keeping Ben for two days. Daniel would take him again at the weekend.

Pablo was down with Ben by the time I stepped back inside, and they were getting straight down to it.

'*No me gusta*,' Ben was saying with as guttural an accent as a ten-year-old Irish boy could muster.

'*No te gusta*, okay, *pero no te gusta que?*' Pablo asked with a cheeky grin.

'What's he saying, Mam?'

'He's saying well done for knowing *no me gusta*, but you need to follow it up with something like... say what it is you don't like.'

'*No me gusta* homework,' Ben said emphatically, and Pablo laughed.

'Clever, *muy listo*, but what's the word for homework?'

'*Momento por favor*,' Ben said and whipped out a tablet, which he swiped to on.

'*Los deberes*,' he said with a triumphant grin.

'*Pues, no te gusta los deberes*,' Pablo said, putting an arm around him. 'You don't like the homework... well, you do good in Spanish though, so you like to study.'

I got Ben to bed early that night and got a good sleep myself. One thing counselling teaches you is that sleep and rest are very important. It's exhausting listening to people all day, and you really want to give them the best attention you can.

Alan was in my ten-to-eleven slot two days later. He still looked breezy and confident, checking the room out like he hadn't been in it before.

'All good?' he asked.

The casual nature of the question made in a formal environment made me think he was trying to defuse the tension and turn it into something he could control. I pictured him conducting so many of his day-to-day affairs in the same matey, casual manner, and I was sure it worked for him. But that wasn't what he was seeing me for, so I wasn't going to play along.

'Yes, thanks. Now, how did you feel after the last session?'

He shrugged and sat down. 'Yeah, grand, not a bother.'

I waited to see if he would follow that up with anything, but he just shrugged again. I could see he was doing his best to look casual and offhand.

'Okay, Alan, in the last session you had been telling me something about your upbringing, and we got to the point where you had told me about your family background. Was there anything you wanted to add to that, or was there anything you thought about in the meantime that you wanted to bring up?'

Alan shifted in his chair and bit his lower lip.

'I thought, after, that maybe I told you too much. What a sob story, eh?'

'But you are here for a reason.'

'Yeah, I suppose.'

Alan was deflecting, torn between his natural outward stance of positivity and bravado and of unveiling the vulnerability within. It was going to take time and patience with him, but that was nothing out of the ordinary. I was confident we would get there eventually.

'What do you think it is?' he asked me suddenly.

'What do I think *what* is?'

'Why I have such a temper, and why I can't have relationships.' He looked at me in a challenging way. 'You're the expert.'

'I can only work with what I get from you. That's why it takes time. It's not a race to come to a conclusion. It's a case of biding our time so we can get to the root cause of it.'

'That's all very well for you to say. It's me who has to live with it.' He shunted forward in his seat so he was closer to me and staring me down.

'I know, and I understand how difficult that can be.'

I could see he needed to blow off a bit of steam – again all part of the process, and I wasn't going to feed it. Eventually he settled down, sat back in his chair, and started talking about the difficulty of bringing himself up and the insecurity he felt beneath the survivor's exterior that he had cultivated.

As we ended the session, I reminded him that he should think about everything he had told me and see if there was anything he had left out. He was walking towards the door when he stopped in his tracks and turned back around to face me.

'Actually there is something else I need to tell you.' He looked at the floor. I waited, but he kept looking down.

'And what is that?' I asked after a long pause.

He shook his head. 'Sorry, it's too personal. I'm not ready to tell you yet.'

'Are you sure?'

He looked up suddenly, and I could see real anger in his eyes. 'I said I'm not ready to tell you yet,' and then he stormed out.

I was a little shaken by the incident, but I brought it to Dorothy in supervision later on.

'He seemed very upset to you?' Dorothy asked. 'Well, that's a normal reaction, isn't it? Our clients get upset all the time. Are you sure you're not getting too involved?'

She was peering at me over her gold-rimmed spectacles. I started fiddling with the ends of my hair – something I do when I am agitated.

'No. I'm not getting too involved. It was just the sudden-ness of it took me by surprise. His whole mood changed so quickly.'

Dorothy took her glasses off, and her clear blue eyes scanned my face.

'Just be certain that he is the right client for you. There are plenty of other therapists who can take him on. You might need a bit more time to get over what you went through.'

'No, he will stay on as my client, and I am in full control of my faculties as a counsellor.' My response was clipped. Dorothy's attitude was starting to annoy me. I didn't like her implying that I was reading too much into Alan's behaviour. I might have been through a traumatic experience, but I still backed myself as a good counselor capable of maintaining neutrality.

'Okay, we'll take it one step at a time, but I'll be keeping a close eye on this one.'

Both irritated and shaken by the chat with Dorothy, I decided to unwind by taking a swim at the local leisure centre. In the evenings, they set out lanes in the pool for more experienced swimmers to do lengths, and that was exactly what I liked to do. Alternating between front crawl and breaststroke, I could easily clock up thirty lengths, lost in the fluid momentum as my body sliced through the warm water. It was a real chance for me to escape from the cerebral machinations of my day job and turn into a mechanical, physical creature immersed in the reverie of sustained, unthinking motion.

Feeling both tired and relaxed afterwards, I drove home. I was going to have a night to myself. Ben was back with Daniel, and Pablo was off meeting friends. Pablo and I were still officially dating, so we made formal arrangements to meet up rather than having him just casually call by. That suited me. I was mad about him, but I wanted to take it nice and slow. Time alone to do whatever I wanted to do was a welcome and precious gift.

I put on some trashy TV and poured a glass of red to have with my dinner. Tired after the swim, the food and the wine, I fell into an easy slumber, waking up just enough to drag myself to the bathroom in the middle of the night. It was then, while washing my hands, that I noticed my opal ring from Daniel was missing.

Curses, I thought. *I must have left it in the changing rooms at the pool.*

But then I thought back through the day and realised I had taken it off a couple of times when I washed my hands. Those opals don't get on with water at all. I planned to call the swimming pool first thing in the morning, and after, I would check the bathroom at work. It must be in one of those two places unless it had just worked its way loose off my finger somewhere.

4

DANIEL

'How's things in the shop?' Pamela asked as soon as I got home.

'Grand, quiet enough but steady,' I replied, trying to put a brave face on things. The quiet enough part was true, the steady bit not quite so true, but I had enough on my mind and was determined to present as positive a face as I could to Pamela.

Pamela had made a spicy bean stew served up with sourdough bread, and that helped make my cheery outlook appear more genuine. 'This is good. Are you sure you shouldn't have gone into catering rather than HR? I can see a serious veggie restaurant with your name on it.'

'It's just cupboard ingredients, and the bread is from that fancy coffee shop down the road, so no kudos to me for that.'

'Lots of kudos, and I like the spices. Didn't know they were lurking in the cupboard.'

'You'd be amazed what a few chili flakes can do,' she said with a broad smile.

Pamela didn't smile often, but when she did, her whole

face lit up. Her dark hair could sometimes make her features look a little harsh, so it was lovely to see her beaming.

I reached a hand across the table to cover hers.

'That spicy food is getting me all heated up.' I checked my watch. 'Hmm, Ben is out on a playdate till eight, so that gives us about an hour. Any ideas?'

'Maybe. I've got college stuff to do, but I guess I can work into the wee hours.'

We tumbled into bed, and I soon forgot the troubles in the shop. As we lay in bed afterwards, Pamela ran a finger across my chest.

'You've got some grey hairs there, darling. All that stress getting to you?'

'Never. Not when I have someone like you to come home to.' I pulled her in closer to me and ran my hand over the gentle curve of her bum.

'You know, I was thinking,' she said slowly. 'If you're up against it at the shop, I'm sure Nicole could cut a bit of slack with the maintenance payments for Ben.'

'Well, he does spend most of his time over there, so that's a reasonable agreement. Anyway, that's something between me and Nicole. You don't need to worry about it.'

Pamela pulled angrily back from me in the bed. 'Well, I think it concerns us all now. You're having difficulties that are causing you stress. Unfortunately I'm not yet in a position to contribute, so we need to be practical.'

'I *am* being practical. It's an arrangement, and I keep my arrangements.' Irritation crept into my voice, and I really didn't want it to spoil our moment. 'Nicole looks after all the school expenses, so I have to put my bit in.'

'She does have a well-paying job, which you don't at the moment.'

That was true, but it really was something between me

and Nicole, so I said nothing. The atmosphere had become heavy between us, and that upset me.

I rolled out of bed and got dressed. 'Ben will be here soon, so we'd better get ready.'

Pamela stayed in bed, looking up at me. 'You're annoyed, aren't you? I was only trying to help.'

I leaned across the bed to kiss her, but it was too late to make amends. The playful mood had evaporated.

Next day in work, I was mulling over what Pamela had said about the maintenance when my phone buzzed with a message. It was an old friend of mine and Nicole's called Pete.

'Daniel, how's it going?' Pete said in his familiar, gravelly baritone voice. With a tone like his, he was well suited for his chosen career as a criminal lawyer.

'Good, yeah. Yourself?' I hadn't heard from Pete for quite a while, a little thrown by the call.

'Not so bad, not so bad. Listen, we've a bit of catching up to do. I wondered if you were around for a coffee?'

'Oh, like when?'

'Today?'

'So soon? You're a fast mover.'

'Yeah, a couple of things to chat to you about. It's been too long. I'm in town, so I can meet you somewhere near your shop.'

'Yeah, sure. I usually grab something around one.'

'1pm it is, then. Text me the name of a place, and I'll be there.'

I texted him the name of a funky little coffee shop around the corner from me, but I wondered what Pete's sudden impulse to have a coffee with me was about. Sure, we had been friends for a long time, so it was probably just him realising it had been quite a while since we'd chatted. But there was something in the urgency of his tone that made me think it might be a little more than that.

At 12.50pm, I was about to shut up shop and put a sign in the window saying 'back in an hour' when a well-dressed young man strolled in, looking carefully over the products on display. I watched him, with his slicked-back brown hair and tweedy sports jacket, as he examined the various bits and pieces. He looked like the sort of customer who might be on the lookout for a thoughtful gift, so I let him take his time. But there was also something about him that was troubling me. He looked familiar, yet I couldn't put my finger on it.

Then he spoke, and I knew exactly who he was.

'You don't recognise me, do you?' he asked, and his voice brought me right back to that terrible day in this very same shop. Except that day, Gary Mulligan had barged in and had been right up in my face before I could react.

I instinctively pulled back and moved towards my phone beside the cash desk.

'It's okay.' Gary smiled. 'No need for phones or drama. I came to say sorry.'

I still kept moving for the phone. He stayed where he was, hands outstretched in a gesture of openness and appeasement.

'Really, hear me out. I'll be gone in a second. I've changed. Everything has changed. I feel terrible for what I did, but I was messed up.'

I kept looking at him, waiting for him to move, but something about the way he stood there – arms open, stance relaxed – made me hesitate. The calm guy before me was a million miles from the red-faced, white-knuckled ball of tension who had confronted me before. On that day, he had burst into the shop, threatening me and disturbing the few customers I had, until I had to call the police to get him forcibly removed. It had scared the hell out of me. I didn't know if the guy had a knife or what. He could have attacked me or, worse, attacked a customer. The injured customer might have sued me and brought my shop dream crashing down.

Back then my skin had prickled with tension, and the hair on the back of my neck had stiffened. Now, looking at him, I felt nothing, just the sense that there was a human in front of me who clearly meant no harm.

Gary smiled as if he had read what was flashing through my mind. 'Like I say, things have changed. I've got my own place and a partner now in London, but it has been bugging me what I put you guys through. I'm back in Dublin for a couple of days, so I had to drop by.'

'Okay, that's good of you, and I appreciate it, but I would ask one thing of you.'

'Anything,' he said, arms open even wider now.

'Don't make any attempt to contact Nicole. I can see you don't mean me any harm, but Nicole won't see it that way. Is that clear?' I could hear anger leaching into my voice as I said that last bit. The trauma of that incident still affected me.

Gary backed off a couple of paces, brought his hands together and held them up in a gesture of appeasement. 'I do understand, Daniel, and you have my word. She's a delicate soul. I know that.'

With that, he turned and walked out of the shop. I stared at the closed door and wondered if I'd hallucinated what had just happened. I would have to tell Nicole – a prospect I didn't relish.

I closed up the shop and took in the sights of the busy city streets, allowing myself to relax again after the encounter. I didn't want to walk in on Pete all tensed up. I could see that Gary had really changed, but seeing him again in the flesh had definitely thrown me.

The café was full of steam and noise when I pushed the door open. Funky artwork plastered the walls, and people were huddled in conversation at the small wooden tables that were dotted around. I spotted Pete in a corner by the window and waved at him before weaving my way through the tables to reach him.

'So how's the form?' Pete stood to greet me.

I hadn't seen him in a couple of years, since before Nicole and I separated. His hair looked thinner, and he had put on a bit of weight.

'Not bad, not bad,' I replied. 'The shop's ticking over. Just waiting for all those needy customers to pile through the door.'

'No shortage of customers for me,' Pete said with a wry smile. He was a criminal lawyer. 'They keep doing what they shouldn't be doing, and they land on my doorstep.'

'So, in a way, you are invested in a dysfunctional society.'

Pete laughed. 'You could say that. I like to think I'm doing the right thing and that everyone gets a fair hearing. Guilty until proven innocent and all that.'

'*Habeus corpus*. Is that the expression?'

'Something like that, but it's gotten a lot more compli-cated these days. A bit like my love life, you might say. Hit and miss to say the least. What about yourself?'

I ran my fingers through my hair. The stubble of my short-brown hair brushed against my fingertips, giving me the confidence that at least I had a full head, unlike Pete.

'Well, you probably heard, myself and Nicole split over a year ago. I guess we just buckled under the pressure. I had the shop, and that wasn't going too well, and then one of Nicole's clients turned really nasty, stalking her and then turning on me. That tipped us over the edge. Nicole just wouldn't see reason until it was too late. I had the guy right in my shop, threatening to smash the place up.'

'That sounds tough, but was that something she could have predicted, given her job? I'm sure plenty of her clients are unstable.'

'Of course, but she refused to see the warning signs. She had seen the guy a couple of times after work, standing across the road from the clinic, staring at her. He was waiting for her to come out. That was creepy, but she kept seeing him.'

Pete nodded. 'I see what you mean.'

'And by the way, the same guy was just in my shop, this time to say sorry,' I added. 'Seems to have reformed, but still put me on edge.'

Pete nodded emphatically, but I saw his legal mind sifting through the rationale of what I was saying and sizing up the evidence.

I continued. 'Anyway, whatever about the rights or wrongs of it, that's what sent us over the edge. To be honest, I think we may have been growing apart, and lots of stuff was getting blown out of proportion, so when that happened, well, that was major.'

Pete fiddled with the handle of his coffee cup and stared at me. I found it disconcerting because it was out of sync with the flow of our conversation. I might have even smiled nervously at him.

'Actually, Daniel, I have something to tell you. It was the reason I wanted to see you today.'

'Sure. What is it?'

Pete looked suddenly very serious, and that put me on edge. I had known Pete since college, and we had spent many dissolute nights together on the hunt for women. That now gave us a good bank of stories to remember, but as we both approached middle age, we had grown apart. I still felt I knew him, but often wondered if it was the Pete of the past that I related to.

'I feel I can tell you this now because you are separated, and to be honest, it's been on my mind for the longest time.' Pete was looking down at his coffee mug now. I could see the top of his head and the thinning wisps of greying hair that arched across his crown.

He took a deep breath before he continued. 'Me and Nicole had a brief fling just before you guys got married. It was one of those things that was over before it started, if you know what I mean... I think she was nervous about the commitment, and I had always fancied her. I mean, she was – is so attractive. She was confiding in me and, well, it just happened. It should never have happened, of course, and that's why I wanted to talk to you today. I had to get it off my chest.'

Pete took a hesitant sip of coffee, looking into the mug, as if all the answers to life's problems lay in there.

When I didn't speak, he continued. 'If it makes any difference, I was the one who instigated it. I took advantage of her need for someone to talk to.'

After a pause, I found my voice.

'I don't know what to say,' was the best I could come up with. 'I suppose I'm grateful you told me. It must have taken some courage. I'm disappointed and maybe a bit shocked, I guess.'

'I don't know if it was courageous of me. It was something I had to do because it was gnawing away at me. Maybe it's just selfish of me to tell you now.'

'No, not at all. I appreciate it.' I heard the words come out of my mouth, but I wasn't sure I meant them. I wasn't sure about anything at all.

I left the café and returned to the shop with the deep sense that the past was still clinging onto me.

Gary had just been in, and Pete had dropped a bombshell. I had hoped the split would give Nicole and I the chance to make a fresh start. We had been through enough and deserved it. After today, I could see that was not going to be easy.

Pete's confession also made me wonder about Nicole's state of mind. Gary had said, 'She's a delicate soul.' What had he seen of her in therapy? Had Nicole presented herself in a certain way? Had she unconsciously led him on?

And of course, that presented a new question – if she had done something like that before, could she do it again?

5

NICOLE

The next day, I took lunch in a park near the practice. I wanted time to think, and it was a peaceful place with a myriad of hidden shelters and where leafy trees dipped low to shade cast-iron park benches.

I took one such bench, coffee and veggie wrap in hand, and listened to the melodic trilling of a blackbird in the branches above. Except for the occasional jogger passing, I was afforded complete peace and quiet. Some of my other colleagues were nervous about coming to the park because a woman had been attacked here a couple of years ago. But I reasoned that an attack could happen anywhere. Once I stayed alert and had my phone at the ready, I figured I was okay.

It gave me time to think about Alan's session and him saying he had something else to tell me, but he wasn't ready yet.

In practice we get quite a few 'doorhandle issues', stuff clients bring up just as they are about to leave the room. Sometimes the issues might be nothing at all; other times they can be the kernel of the problem. It can be the one great fear or incident the client can't face up to.

In Alan's case, I suspected that might be his issue. He was a man who comported himself in a particular way, every response carefully measured to give the right outward appearance. He was somebody who thought things through and somebody who liked to stay in control. If he had something he wanted to tell me but wasn't ready to, then I was quietly confident the admission was going to be big. The way his anger flared so quickly whenever I tried to probe made me even more certain. But I was going to have to wait to find out until he was ready to tell me.

Just as I was about to leave, my phone burst into life, and I saw Daniel's name come up on-screen. It was his day to have Ben over, so I worried there might be a problem.

I answered the phone straight away. 'Daniel?'

'Nicole, are you able to talk for a minute?'

'Yes, I'm on lunch.'

'It's just... I had someone come into the shop this morning.'

I felt like cracking a joke and saying *well, it is a shop after all*, but I resisted. There was an urgency in his tone.

'Oh, like who?'

'Don't panic now when I tell you, but it was Gary.'

I did panic. How could I not?

Gary, the stalker, who had followed me home, watched me at work, left me notes, somehow got my phone number and sent me creepy texts and then, when I wasn't responding to his texts, started getting more and more threatening. Finally, having no luck with me, he had gone to Daniel's shop to attack him.

'He's changed,' I heard Daniel say, but the words didn't sink in.

I grabbed my bag and started walking quickly from the park.

Daniel continued. 'Okay, I know it's hard to believe after what happened, but I think he's changed. He came to say sorry. He didn't want to go anywhere near you, so he came to me instead. He really has changed, Nicole.'

I had reached my workplace and slipped in through the heavy, wooden door at the side of the building to access my office on the ground floor. Once I was inside, I closed the door and sat hard on one of the chairs.

'What do you mean he's changed?' I looked out the big bay window that looks onto the gravel car park at the front of the building.

'Listen, Nicole, sorry for ringing you. I'd prefer to be saying this in person, but I won't see you till tomorrow. I was just worried in case, maybe, he did decide to contact you and apologise, and you panicked.'

'Of course I would have panicked – and called the police straight away.'

'Well, you wouldn't need to,' Daniel said. 'That was my first reaction too, once I knew who it was, but he seemed really sincere. I'm a good judge of people, Nicole. Before he left though, I told him not to go near you. He might still feel like apologising, but I made it clear he wasn't to approach you.'

Was Daniel a good judge of character? In that moment, I didn't know if I agreed with him on that. I considered him to be a bit innocent at times, but then he often thought the same of me.

'That's good of you to say that to him,' I said, 'but how can we be so sure he won't try to contact me? Maybe he's playing a double bluff or something. He's a complex character. I know. I counselled him.'

'I know, Nicole, but it's really what I felt. We can never be sure; that's the only certainty.'

I hung up and did some breathing exercises so I could get in the right frame of mind for my next client. Images of Gary kept popping into my head throughout the afternoon, but I eventually started to relax and put my trust in Daniel's judgement.

Pablo was due over at my place around eight that evening, so I got a quick swim in after I got home. It gave me a chance to ask the staff at the pool about my missing opal ring. But they hadn't seen it, so that was one place I could rule out.

Then as I got close to my own house – in fact as I turned into my drive – I got a shout from my neighbour James. He was at his front door, leaning out of it to wave at me. The action gave him a kind of comical appearance, like the archetypal nosey neighbour waiting for a chance to engage. Except from what I knew of James, he was anything but the nosey neighbour. He was a young, good-looking guy in his early thirties who worked in advertising. He had a retro style with brightly coloured, tight-fitting, old-fashioned clothes that made me think of Pee-wee Herman, except James had a well-sculpted body and a breezy, urbane air that killed any Pee-wee comparisons.

He walked towards me, holding what looked like a letter in his hand. It wasn't uncommon for post to end up in the wrong house. He leaned across the low, white picket fence that separated our gardens, his arm outstretched.

'Nicole,' he said with a diffident smile, 'em, this was posted in my letterbox when I got home.'

I could see now it was not an envelope but a single sheet of coloured paper, with gold and silver glitter dusted across the top. There was a message on it, scrawled messily in red and green marker. It looked like something a young child might put together.

Then I read the message.

In the childish, coloured writing it said, 'Love you forever, James. N.'

I frowned at it, trying to figure out why this dashing young man would be showing me such a thing. Then it slowly dawned on me.

'Oh,' I said, and felt myself flushing. 'You think I wrote this?' I went to hand it back, but he didn't take it.

'I wasn't sure,' said James. 'It's not April Fool's, is it?'

'No, absolutely not. I've been at work all day, so I wouldn't have been here to deliver it.' James looked at my wet hair and the sports bag over my shoulder. 'Oh... I just dropped home quickly to get these and went straight back out to the pool.'

'I'm sure it's nothing,' he said. 'Just a bit on the odd side. People could get the wrong impression.'

I wasn't sure what to say to that, so we just stood there for a few awkward seconds before he turned and walked away. I was left alone with the childish note in my hand. The way he left me with it only reinforced his assumption that the note had come from me.

I went into my house feeling puzzled. All fresh feelings of relaxation the swim left me with had evaporated. The note was odd, no doubt about that, but it had nothing to do with me. It was signed N, not Nicole.

Did he think I fancied him? My God, after all the trouble I'd gone through with my split from Daniel, how could he? And I was seeing someone.

When Pablo arrived, I showed it to him.

'Cute,' he said, wrinkling his nose at the glitter and the childish writing.

'Or not,' I said. 'James thinks I wrote it.'

Pablo laughed loudly. He had a kind of guttural, chesty laugh due to his smoker's lungs. 'You? You fancy him? He's not bad looking, you know,' Pablo teased.

I tried to snatch the note from him, miffed that he wasn't taking it seriously enough.

'You want, I could give it him again?' Pablo said. 'Maybe he didn't get the message first time.'

'There is no message,' I said, enunciating each word clearly, but seeing Pablo's mischievous smile, I started laughing before I got to the end of the sentence. After all, who could take something like a badly crafted note seriously?

We had a nice night then, watching *First Dates* on TV and drinking a fairly robust Rioja that Pablo had brought. I managed to put thoughts of the note behind me. I did think about Gary though as I lay in bed and dawn neared. I envied Pablo his ability to sleep well. He always managed it. Anxiety – I know from my profession and from personal experience – is what tends to keep us awake. Gary was probing the borders of my anxiety. If he had come to reconcile and make peace, it was a bit too soon after traumatising us.

Leaving the next morning, I was surprised to see James standing at the small picket fence that divided our properties. He was staring at a hole in the fence; a couple of the wooden lattes hung loose from the rest of the fence.

'Oh,' I remarked as he tried to push them back into place.

He looked up at me, and I have to say, there was very little warmth in the look. 'Someone took a mind to smash a bit of the fence on my side.'

He put extra emphasis on the word *my*, like he was not so subtly pointing out that it was on his side and not on mine. That threw me.

'Could have been a stray dog or fox or something,' I said, rooting for ideas as to what might actually be big enough to cause that sort of damage.

'If it was an animal,' James said tersely.

'Oh, but what else?' I was genuinely puzzled. 'Maybe teenagers?' We'd had problems occasionally with high-spirited – meaning drunken – teenagers running through the gardens, but that had been a good while back.

James stood suddenly and said, 'There's more than this. It gets worse.'

He marched over to the hidden side of his pristine Prius and fetched something from underneath the driver's side. As he approached, I could see it was a badly damaged wing mirror from his car.

'Oh no,' I said. 'That's going to cost a right few quid. That's terrible.'

'It is,' he said matter-of-factly, and then, strangely, he started rooting in his trouser pocket. 'I also found this nearby, beside the broken mirror, in fact.'

He handed me something small and light, and when I opened my hand and saw what it was, it made my blood run cold.

It was the engagement ring I had lost, the one with the opal.

6

DANIEL

I got a call from a number I didn't recognise as I was dusting and arranging stock in my shop. At first I just stared at the phone. The incident with Gary was still playing on my mind. Okay, he did seem to have genuinely turned a corner, but after what he had done before, I really didn't know if he could be trusted.

I let the phone ring, knowing within a ring or two it would just go to voicemail. But maybe whoever it was wouldn't leave a voicemail. Maybe it was something to do with my business. I answered and heard a familiar voice speak, but I couldn't place it.

'Daniel?' The person spoke with urgency. I immediately got a bad feeling.

'Yes? Who is this?'

'It's me, James from next door.'

That sentence made little sense until I got the context of 'next door'. It was our neighbour from when Nicole and I lived together. Cool, man-about-town James who drove funky cars and liked his fashion.

'James, how are you?'

We had exchanged phone numbers, to use for emergencies whenever we were away on holidays. We had a reciprocal 'keep an eye on the house and put the bins out' arrangement.

'I'm okay, Daniel. Sorry for calling at this hour and out of the blue, but I wanted to talk to you about something.'

That really got me worried. James liked to keep his business to himself and exuded the aura of one who definitely had his act together.

'It's Nicole. I don't know how to say this, but some strange stuff happened around my house, and I think she may have had something to do with it.'

'Oh?'

'Don't get me wrong, Daniel. It's not that I want to apportion blame or hold her to account for anything. I just thought I should let you know.'

'What sort of things are we talking about?' I could feel my instinct to defend Nicole kicking in.

'There was a note posted in my door from somebody. A romantic note, and it was signed with the initial N.'

'Okaaay, but what makes you think it's Nicole?'

My defence of Nicole kicked in even more. I mean, so what? It was a note.

'But that could have been anyone, James. Could be some of the local teens messing. Maybe one of them even fancies you.' I finished with a laugh. That was a scenario I could easily imagine: James with his fancy threads and straight, fair hair that he wore over his eyes.

'There was more, Daniel. The fence was broken overnight as well, on my side only, and then to trump it all, the wing mirror on my Prius was smashed.'

'But why would Nicole embark on a campaign of vandalism like that?' I was starting to get irritated. What had this all to do with Nicole, and who did he think he was throwing accusations around like that?

'I know it all sounds unconnected, and I really wasn't sure myself, but then I found the ring just beside my car.'

'The ring?'

'Nicole's engagement ring, the one with the opal. I remember it clearly from when you guys were together because it was the only piece of jewelry Nicole wore.'

That was true. Nicole wasn't one for wearing jewelry, but she was attached to that ring. I had noticed that even after we split, she still wore it all the time. It had given me some peace of mind when I'd seen it on her. It made me remember that there had been plenty of good things about our relationship, even though it had fallen apart in the end.

'Are you sure, James?' I think I said that just to buy time. There was no way he would come out with something so definite if he wasn't sure.

'Yes, I'm sure, Daniel. I gave her back the ring this morning. She looked surprised. I'm really sorry to be telling you all this, but I thought it was best.'

James knew about the incident with Gary Mulligan and about how it had driven Nicole to the edge of a complete breakdown.

'I'm not looking for anything to be done about this, Daniel. Maybe it wasn't Nicole, as you say, but I wanted to let you know. Better safe than sorry. We'll keep this between ourselves.'

I could tell he was genuinely acting out of concern. He wasn't looking for anything to be done, and we would keep it between ourselves.

'Okay, James, thanks for letting me know. I'll keep an eye.'

I didn't want to immediately stir things up by calling Nicole. It did make me worry about her mental state though. Was she still suffering from PTSD, and was it making her unstable?

Ben would be staying with me later, and I would be dropping him at Nicole's the next day. That would give me time to figure out the best way to broach this with her. Even better, Nicole might bring it up herself. It was while I was thinking of this and the fact that Ben would be staying over later that the beginnings of an idea started to form.

That evening, I put my idea into action.

'Ben,' I said to him once he had finished his homework and was playing a game on a handheld console.

'Yeah?' he replied without looking up.

'Oh, nothing, really.' I sat in beside him on the couch. 'I just wanted to check you're sleeping properly and looking after yourself while over at your mam's. It's important, you know, for a growing kid like you.'

'Of course I am,' he said, still not looking up from his game.

'To sleep well, it's important you feel safe, isn't it?'

Ben shrugged. 'Yeah, I guess.'

'You'd tell me if you didn't feel safe, wouldn't you?'

'Of course. Or I'd tell Mam.'

'You would, of course. And you'd let me know if there was ever anything that was worrying you while you were there, if you saw anything that you thought was a bit funny.'

Ben twisted the console until it was at an obtuse angle, then started banging his finger on one of the control buttons. A bunch of laser-guided missiles started streaking across the screen.

'Sure, Dad,' he said, almost breathless with the effort of concentration.

Then he stopped playing, put the console down and looked up at me. 'Dad, do you want me to be a spy?'

I laughed and tickled him, and he scrunched right up against me. 'No, of course not. Well, unless you wanted to be a spy.'

'Yeah, that sounds like fun. I do, Dad. I want to be a spy.'

Later, when Ben had gone to bed, Pamela and I settled on the couch with a couple of glasses of red wine. I had my arm draped over her shoulder. We were watching some show where an architect was blabbing on about the amazing things he was going to do to with a regular two-up two-down house. The couple who owned the house kept sneaking glances at each other like it was all too good to be true. The show was starting to irritate me. I had a lot on my mind.

Pamela must have read that mind because she leaned back to look at me.

'Jealous?' she asked.

I must have had a startled look on my face because Pamela laughed.

'Jealous of those two on the telly, you plonker. What did you think I was talking about?'

'Jealous? No. There are a bunch of other negative feeling vying for my attention, but not jealousy.'

'Yeah, likewise, these programmes can all be a bit same-y. So what are you thinking about?'

I instinctively looked back to check that Ben hadn't snuck out of his bedroom.

'It's... actually, it's a couple of things. There's a bit of weird shit going on.'

Pamela sat up. 'Sounds interesting. Do go on.'

'Well, I got a call from Nicole's neighbour James, and he said some strange things happened around his house. And that he found Nicole's engagement ring close to where the stuff happened.'

Pamela's eyes widened. 'So he thinks she was involved? What kind of stuff?'

I told her about the car, the fence, the note. She seemed most shocked by the love note.

'You think she really could have done something like

that? Like she fancies the guy, or she's trying to get his attention or something?'

'No. I don't know. I just don't know. There was something
else as well. I got a call from Pete, an old friend. We met for
coffee, and he told me that he and Nicole had a quick fling
just before we got married.'

Pamela scrunched up her features. 'Oh, that's not a very
nice thing to hear.'

'No, it wasn't, but, you know, hearing the two things in the
one day, even though they happened far apart, it makes me
wonder if she's okay, you know. Like, if she's ever been okay.
Do I actually know her?'

Pamela shook her head. 'I didn't want to say, but I've often
had my doubts about her. The fling though. Do you think it
stopped before the engagement?'

'I think so,' but even as I said it, I didn't know for sure.

'It's just Ben. You know. The maintenance.'

'What do you mean?'

A look of deep concern shrouded Pamela's features. 'Don't
get me wrong now, but you are you completely sure he's
yours? I mean, say if the affair went on even longer, like when
you were married.'

I slammed my wine glass down on the coffee table in
front of me.

'How can you say a thing like that? That's horrible. Of
course he's mine. That's outrageous. I was just saying I was
worried about Nicole, but you had to bring this whole other
dimension into it. It was a quick fling, and then it was over.
Why would Pete tell me today if it was anything more than
that? That's not on, Pamela.'

I stormed off to our bedroom and lay on the bed.

The conversation with Pamela was replaying mercilessly
in my head. How could she suggest something like that? Ben

meant so much to me. The very thought of what she was implying cut right through my love for him.

I took some deep breaths. It had just been a thought. It did not mean anything.

Pamela slipped in to the room shortly after and slid in behind me on the bed, pulling herself in close and wrapping her arm around me.

'I'm sorry, love. That just kind of came out. I just worry about the financial stress you are under. It's not easy for you. I understand that.'

I think the two of us must have fallen asleep then, because I woke with lights still seeping in from the hallway. It took me a while to get my bearings and to remember all the news I had been hit with.

I had a lot to think about.

I hoped a good night's sleep would give me some fresh perspective.

7

NICOLE

The opal ring was the thing that bothered me most about all this. The weird stuff with James could have been just that if it hadn't been for the ring showing up. That made it a deliberate action on someone's part.

Unless, of course, I had lost the ring somewhere outside the front of my house. Maybe it had gotten tangled up in a towel when I was getting out of the pool, or maybe I had slipped it in my jacket pocket while washing my hands at work, and then it had slipped from my pocket as I climbed out of the car. I usually took my jacket off when driving and carried it into the house draped over my bag. Carried like that, the ring could have easily slipped out.

The first problem was I didn't usually put it in my jacket pocket, and second, the ring had made its way over to the damage on James's car. It didn't add up. The most likely scenario was the one I didn't want to contemplate: somebody had taken my ring and deliberately put it there to implicate me in what had happened.

That thought played heavily on my mind at work the next

day. Who would do that and why? It seemed like an act of petty revenge. Was Gary involved? Could he possibly be? How would he get access to the ring? Was he watching me again? Did he see the ring fall and then put the plan in place?

It all seemed unlikely, given Daniel's recent impression of him, but if it wasn't him, then who?

I had some time to go through my files before the first client of the day. I pulled Alan's file out. His case had been on my mind. A trauma of some sort was at the root of his problems, but what type of trauma and from where? He had been brought up in the care system and allowed to run wild on the streets, so the possibilities for its cause were endless. Then there was his home life – alcoholic parents who were unable to look after him. Who knew what bad people visited the house while he was there?

It brought me back to my own childhood, as these cases often did. I had gone through extensive counselling of my own before I'd been allowed to practice, and that had exposed my own trauma.

I had an alcoholic father, just like Alan. A loud, abusive man with an easily triggered temper. Everyone had to walk on eggshells, never knowing when the next blow would come. In response, I had become a pleaser, trying to keep the peace, but all the time the anger burned at me. The true nature of that anger had never seen the light of day, not until the day Gary started stalking me, and when it did manifest, I had been shocked. Gary had never known how lucky he was. He had escaped with his life – by a whisker.

He had pushed me to a place I had never been before. I had felt a cold, white rage overcome me, and he'd been the target. He had backed me into a corner, and the full scale of my trauma had been unleashed. The feeling that had flooded through me had been otherworldly, like it was outside of my control. It had given me a solemn sense of purpose. I had been in danger. The danger had to be eliminated. No ambivalence. No feelings.

Gary had been a client, so I'd known a lot about him. He liked to go to the gym in the evenings. He walked home. I had waited outside his apartment block, a steel bar gripped in my hands. I hadn't felt nervous. I'd felt nothing but the cold, white rage in me. He was about to be seriously hurt. He deserved it. But just as I'd emerged from my hiding place, a group of young revellers had burst out the door of his apartment. They'd stayed there, messing about, giddy with the promise of the night ahead, while Gary pushed past them and entered the safety of the foyer.

After that, I knew my own trauma was still there, and it scared the crap out of me. The person who had appeared for that brief time was someone I didn't know, someone from my past who was still buried inside me, and it made me question everything.

Daniel and I had split soon after. I had been getting more and more temperamental, getting really snappy with him. I could see how it had been affecting him, and I knew I had to let him go. He'd thought it was because of the trauma of the stalking. He'd also known about my troubled family life. Daniel had been sympathetic, but I never told him the real reason for the break-up.

I had been scared – of myself and what I might do.

I had gone back for more counselling. I had started doing yoga, mindfulness, meditation, swimming, doing anything that might help me understand my trauma, but I had never told anyone about what I had planned for Gary.

I blinked away the memories and looked at Alan's notes, wondering when he would be ready to tell me his terrible secret. I wanted to help him, but I knew I would have to wait until he was ready. He had to trust me enough to let me see

into the darkest recesses of his soul. The day would come.
Meanwhile, I would work on building that trust.

I worked late that day, having had a long list of clients. I
texted Daniel to let him know I would be late, because he was
dropping Ben over. Pablo would still be teaching.

The rest of the counsellors in the building had gone by
six, so it was just me, and that suited me fine. I was able to
concentrate on my paperwork and nip out to the kitchen to
get a cup of tea without fear of getting tangled up in some
conversation. I wanted to get home, heat up a bit of dinner for
Ben and then settle in to helping him with his homework.

Dusk was falling as I finished the last of my client notes
and checked on the list for the next day. I had a small lamp
on in my office, just enough light to work by. It threw
shadows around the airy, Georgian room with its stucco
ceiling work and corner-positioned cherubic angels blowing
what looked like kisses to each other. I was idly looking up at
one of those angels, lost in thought, when I heard a
scratching noise on the sash window that looked out onto the
gravel car park at the front of the property. Those windows
were notoriously shaky and prone to making noise, so I
ignored it. I started to pack up, when I saw the dusk was
quickly turning to darkness. As I shuffled the papers into
their cardboard manila files, I heard the same scratching
noise again. This time it was sharper and more pronounced.

Quietly, I cursed those windows. They looked great from
the outside but were so shaky and draughty. Because the
building was listed, there was a preservation order on everything, so nothing could be done about the original windows.
They weren't going anywhere. Sometimes birds banged off
them, but that was usually in the daytime when they saw
their own reflections.

The noise that I had heard was sharper than a bird.

Whatever it was could wait till tomorrow.

But there it was again.

Sharp, distinct, like something hitting off the window. This time I could find no excuse for it. Not a bird, not a gust of wind shaking the window. No, this was something else, and it was coming at regular intervals. Again, another hit, this time with a cracking sound, like there was more force being applied.

I knocked off the lamp and peered outside. The car park was cast into dusky shadow, but nothing was visible, just the outline of my car standing alone.

A shiver ran through me. I stood stock-still and listened. Was that the sound of gravel crunching in the car park? Was somebody moving out there?

There, again, the sound of something hitting off the window. A stone. I was sure it was a stone. Somebody was taking gravel from the car park and throwing it against the window. Somebody knew I was inside and alone.

Fear turned to anger. Someone was targeting me and trying to scare me. I tugged the top half of the sash window down.

'Who's out there? What are you playing at? I'm calling the police.'

Silence.

I shut the window as quickly as I had opened it. The rush of cool, evening air had made me feel momentarily exposed.

The second I shut the window, a bright, broad beam of light flashed into my face, blinding me, forcing me back a few paces and to shield my eyes. The anger disappeared as quickly as it had appeared. Panic started to set in. The beam invaded the property like an intruder.

Whoever was outside had this planned. First the stones, then my reaction, then the blinding beam of light. What had they planned next?

I reached for my phone. Pablo was at work. He would be

in the middle of giving a class. He had told me before that he usually left his phone in the staff room during class time so he wouldn't be interrupted.

I called Daniel. It went to voicemail.

Shit, I thought. *He's probably just on his way home now.* Daniel was an absolute stickler for the rule that there was no place for phones while driving. He had often given out about the young people he saw driving with their phones in their laps, looking up every now and then to check the road in front of them. 'Absolutely reckless, selfish behaviour,' he had said.

I texted him.

> *Please pick up. Fast. I'm at work. There's somebody outside. I'm scared.*

I didn't know what to do. Whoever was out there had me at their mercy. Maybe I should call the police. But what if it was just somebody messing about? What could I say to the police? That there was somebody throwing stones up at my window, and they had a torch? As a counsellor, I had a professional reputation to uphold. I didn't want my state of mind scrutinized.

The beam of light was trained exactly in the centre of the window. I shielded my eyes again and opened the top part once more.

'Whoever you are, there is somebody on their way to get me now. You're going to be done for harassment and intimidation.'

I closed the window and waited. A small shower of stones slapped against the window, making a series of sharp raps when they hit. I jumped back and cowered in the corner of the room. The next stones might smash the glass, and then what? The person out there would be able to get in.

I had to call the police. I didn't care.

I grabbed for my phone and, with fingers that were stiff and uncompliant with tension, I pulled up the number pad. Just as I did, my phone sprang into life, startling me so much that I dropped it. Picking it up, I saw Daniel's name splashed across the screen.

'Daniel,' I whispered.

'What is it, Nicole? What's going on?'

'I'm at work. There's someone outside. They're throwing stones at my office window. They have a torch. I'm alone here. I'm scared, Daniel.'

'Stay where you are. Don't move. I'll be straight over.'

The phone went dead, and I was left to look once more at the intrusive beam that was lighting up the sash window. It held steady, keeping me trapped, isolated, fearful. Whoever was doing this knew exactly what they were doing. This had been well planned. They had waited for the right moment, until my car was the only one in the car park. I sat hunched over in the far corner of my office. No way was I moving or showing myself before Daniel came.

The beam of light moved. I heard gravel crunch in the car park. I stopped breathing and listened. What next? Footsteps, definite footsteps. The light appeared to get stronger. Whoever was out there was getting closer. I could hear the gravel crunch like it was only feet away from me. Then the footsteps stopped.

I gulped a quick breath and held it. Silence followed. The beam held steady against the back wall of my office. It was like it was a live, intelligent presence, seeking me out.

Then, mercifully, I heard the sound of a car speeding up the road. The beam disappeared as quickly as it had come. I heard the sound of someone hurrying across the gravel. I ran to the window to see Daniel's car swing into the car park, and at the same time, a dark figure disappeared out a pedestrian gate to the side of the car park.

I pulled the top part of the window down and shouted, 'Daniel, they've gone out the other gate.'

It was hopeless though. Daniel was still in the car and couldn't hear me. He screeched to a halt, sending a spray of gravel flying across the car park. Jumping from the car, he left the door open and the engine running and ran straight over to bang on the outside door. I hurried down and pulled it open to see him looking pale and frantic.

'What happened. Where are they?' he asked breathlessly.

'They've gone. Someone slipped out the side gate when they saw your car.'

Daniel turned to survey the car park. It was perfectly still and quiet apart from the gentle purr of his car's engine. He turned back to me and put a strong arm around me, pulling me in close. My heart was hammering in my chest. I was sure he could feel it.

'It's okay,' he said over and over. The words were like a soothing mantra; I was hypnotized by their calming effect.

We stood there for a full five minutes. His car engine idled. There was no other sound or movement. Whoever it was had vanished.

'Who would do something like that?' Daniel asked eventually.

'I don't know. I really don't, but the stuff that was going on with James. I mean, are they linked? Is it the same person? It must be, but what do they want? To scare the crap out of me? Well, it's working. I'm scared, Daniel. I don't like this. Not after what happened before. I don't think I can take anything like that again.'

Daniel walked me to my car. I sat in it, and my hands were shaking as I fumbled for my keys.

'Are you okay to drive? I'll stick close to you all the way to your place. I'll be right behind you.'

'Yeah, I'll manage. Thanks.'

Daniel stayed beside my car until I started the engine. I could see him looking around the car park. I followed his gaze and saw nothing but the shadows across the gravel cast by trees.

I wonder if he believes me, I thought, *or if he thinks it's me being stressed and overreacting after he told me that Gary had been in to see him.*

I waited till he was back in his car and right behind me before I drove out the gate that led from the car park and onto the street. It was a quiet street in a residential part of town, big detached houses with looming deciduous trees hanging so low they blocked out the yellowish hue of the street lights. Worried the dark figure could emerge from any of the multitude of shadows, I put my foot on the accelerator and took off up the street. Daniel followed close behind.

I didn't want to think about what had just happened as I drove, because I was afraid I might seize up. It would have to wait till I got home, until I was settled on the couch with Pablo, feeling nice and secure. I did my best to block it out and concentrate on driving. Getting home was the priority. Daniel would be dropping Ben over later. Me, Ben and Pablo would be watching something silly on TV later. Everything would be okay again.

I pulled into my drive a few minutes later with my heart still pounding. Daniel pulled up on the street outside, got out and walked over to me.

'Are you okay to go in now?' he asked. 'I can stay with you a while if you like.'

'No, it's okay, but thanks. You need to get Ben and bring him over. I'll be fine now, get myself a nice cup of tea and put some music on.'

I watched him get back in his car and pull off. Instinctively I checked up and down the street before turning for the
door of my house. As I walked past my car, something caught
my attention. There was a scrunched-up piece of paper stuck
under one of the windscreen wipers.

Strange, I thought, *must be one of those advertising flyers.*

But it looked very homemade and uneven. I pulled the
wiper back, took the paper out and unfolded it. As I did, I saw
something had been roughly handwritten on it.

In thick, black ink were the words:

watching you

8

DANIEL

The incident with Nicole really threw me. I tried to play it down with her because I could see she was already spooked, but it left me with a lot of questions. Who might be doing this to her? Why now? Could it be Gary? Had that apology in the shop all been an act to throw me off the scent?

But no, it made no sense. If he was going to stalk Nicole again, the last thing he would do was show up in my shop. Unless, of course, he wanted to get at me. Maybe he felt I was to blame for him getting caught last time. It was me who'd called the police when he'd come to my shop that day.

Either way it worried me. There were two distinct scenarios playing in my mind. The call from my old neighbour James had precipitated one of those scenarios. Was Nicole acting irrationally and turning her attention to James, damaging his property and leaving him that strange note? Was this some after-effect from her earlier trauma with Gary? Could she be looking for attention in some desperate way? Had the incident at her workplace merely been an extension of this demand for attention?

Scenario two was that someone was doing this to her. Worse, they were trying to make it look like she was unhinged, to the extent that she was stalking her neighbour and damaging his property. This second scenario seemed less likely. Who would be doing that to her and why?

I had to wonder if she had lost control of her senses. I had heard that PTSD works in strange ways and that a part of the brain can become disconnected to the point that you can have autonomous regions in your brain doing their own thing. I prayed that wasn't the case, but at the same time, if it was, that really concerned me. My son was staying with her. Was she in a fit state to look after him? I wanted to be able to support Nicole in whatever way I could, but I had to think of Ben as well.

I voiced those concerns to Pamela over dinner after I had told her about the incident at Nicole's work.

'You've got to think about yourself and about Ben,' she said. 'I know you have your concerns about Nicole, and that's admirable, but there is more to her than meets the eye. Take the affair with Pete. What was that about? Do you think Nicole likes to present her vulnerable side to the world, but really she is quite capable of getting what she wants?'

'That's not a very kind reading of the situation.'

'Perhaps not, but maybe it's a realistic one. You know, this course I am doing for HR has taught me a thing or two. One common misconception about HR is that it's all cute and cuddly. It's not. It's about efficiency, and at the end of the day, we're trained to see a situation for what it really is. You are seeing the situation with Nicole through rose-tinted glasses because you have a history there and because, basically, you're a nice guy, a bit of a softie even.'

It wasn't the first time I had been called a softie. It was one of the things Nicole had said to me when I opened my shop. She had accused me of being too nice for the cut and thrust of retail. I believed that if I had a good product that was well made and sold it for a good price, it didn't matter how soft I was. People would buy it, and the money would prove her wrong.

I toyed with a stem of broccoli on my plate and watched it slide elusively, resisting the attention of my fork.

'Maybe you have a point,' I said eventually, 'but I want to give Nicole the benefit of the doubt. She has been through a tough time – that much I know, because I bore witness to it.'

'Well, you could test her reaction to something that you know happened, for example, the fling she had with Pete. If you introduce that topic in a roundabout way, see how she reacts to it. It might tell you a lot about how she is reacting to other things in her life.'

'Maybe,' I said, 'but like I said, I know she has been through quite a bit. I want to help her if she is going through some sort of breakdown.'

'Yes, but you have to think about yourself too and about Ben.'

Pamela was right about that much. Ben was a priority. If there was some prolonged instability there, I needed to know.

The next day after work I had to collect Ben. I called to Nicole's house and asked her if we could have a quick word.

'How are you after yesterday?' I asked.

She blew out a breath. 'Creeped out by the whole thing, to be honest.'

'I'm not surprised. Must have been scary being all alone like that. Who do you think it was?'

'I really don't know. I mean, Gary was the first person who came to mind. Then there's another new client – I can't give his name, but he's young, maybe the same age as Gary – and he's got these unresolved anger issues. I don't think it could be him though. It just doesn't feel right.'

'Did Gary feel right?'

'No, but it made sense once we found out what he was up to.'

'Hindsight then, Nicole. It's the present you need to focus on.'

Nicole took a step back when I said that. She looked surprised. 'Like how?'

'Well, I don't know. Is there anyone else who might hold a grudge or feel hard done by?'

Nicole still looked puzzled. She had this way of playing with loose strands of hair when she was thinking something over.

'Listen, I'll cut to the chase. I got a call from our old friend Pete.' I let that information sink in. Nicole stopped playing with her hair.

'He told me what happened between you two just before we got married.'

Nicole shook her head and looked down at her feet. 'I'm sorry. He shouldn't have done that.' Nicole looked behind, as if to check that Ben wasn't within earshot. She pulled the front door over so it was almost completely closed.

'Shouldn't have done what?'

'Told you. It was just a one-off, and it was a mistake. I was in a vulnerable state at the time. There was a lot going on, stuff I didn't want to tell you about.'

'Well, maybe you should have.' Even though the affair was in the past, I couldn't help but feel a sting of betrayal at the way I'd found out.

'I couldn't. I'm sorry, Daniel, really, I am, but I just couldn't.'

'Couldn't or wouldn't? Maybe it didn't suit you to. Maybe you were happy to string Pete or me along, playing the two of us off each other.'

'It wasn't like that.' Nicole's voice rose in anger.

'What I'm thinking is maybe you were playing too many games, and now look where it's got us.'

'I wasn't playing games. You don't understand.' Nicole was quite loud now.

I turned to see if anybody was around. Sure enough, I saw James, his wife and their little kid in a buggy turning into their drive, coming back from a walk.

Nicole saw them at the same time, and she flushed under the light from the porch. She moved away from me, and before I could say or do anything, she was calling over to James.

'That wasn't me, James, who wrote the note and broke the wing mirror on your car,' she said. 'I don't know who it was, but it wasn't me. I'd never do a thing like that. Someone is trying to set me up, to make me look like a stalker.'

I saw James glance quickly at his wife, a young woman with a perfect bob of auburn hair and eyebrows that were plucked to within an inch of their life. She said nothing, just gave James a look and nodded towards their front door. The pair walked quickly up their drive and disappeared into the sanctuary of their home.

'Oh God, what the hell is happening to me?' Nicole asked. She was holding her head in her hands. I went over and rested her head against my shoulder.

'It's okay, it'll work out. We'll figure out what's going on.' I looked up and saw Ben standing at the door. He was watching us. How long he had been there, I didn't know.

'Hey, Ben,' I said. I was trying to sound cheery, but my voice sounded thin and weak. 'You got your stuff? Ready to come over? There's a nice pepperoni pizza in the oven with your name on it.'

Ben reached behind him into the hall and grabbed his schoolbag, as well as the little duffel bag he used for overnight stays. He dragged both over to me and laid them at my feet.

'Okay, let's go, then,' I said, still trying to maintain the cheery tone.

Nicole reached down to kiss Ben goodbye, and after, he followed me to the car. It felt like we were going through the usual machinations of the everyday routine, but there was a tension and an awkwardness to it that was dragging the ritual down.

9

NICOLE

I was still in shock from the events of the previous day and was no closer to figuring out who might be behind it. But I had no doubt that someone was playing with me, someone with malevolent intent.

I had been so happy when Pablo had arrived home last night. I was able to go back over the events with him once Ben had gone to bed. There had been a certain catharsis in being able to explain my ordeal to a sympathetic audience – something I was aware of from my own counselling practice. Pablo had been sympathetic, but he went quickly on the offensive once I had finished.

'That's so bad, doing something like that to a woman on her own. What kind of person do a thing like that? Nasty. Nasty. That person need themselves sorted out.' He slapped the back of one hand with the palm of the other.

I smiled and rubbed his hand. 'No, as I've said before, revenge gets us nowhere. We need to find out who it is though. I can't go through what I went through before. I just can't. How can I work if I'm afraid? How would I look after my clients?'

'No, you can't. We gonna find whoever this is, don't you worry.'

But I did worry, and worry, as I knew well from my clients, could interfere with a lot of facets of consciousness – concentration being one of them.

At work I found it hard to focus fully. At times, I heard my clients' voices as something distant, almost like they were in another room relating their stories to somebody else. I knew it wasn't fair to them, but all I could do was promise myself that the situation would be resolved quickly. And when it was, my clients would have my full and complete attention again.

Alan was one of my morning clients. I made a special effort to focus on him even though I was distracted.

'How have you been since our last session?' I asked him.

He shrugged his shoulders and ran his hands the length of his thighs, like he was smoothing out some creases.

'Okay, I guess. I'm still not ready to tell you that thing I mentioned last time, so don't get your hopes up.'

'It's not about me getting my hopes up. It's about you feeling safe to disclose whatever it is that you want.'

'Well, maybe I don't feel safe. Big lad like me, you'd think I would, wouldn't you? Doesn't always work like that though, does it?'

'Absolutely not. We all have our face that we show to the world, but what goes on inside is a different matter.'

'Maybe I need a mother. What do you think about that?'

'Would that make you feel more secure?'

'Well, my own mother didn't do a very good job. She was too busy taking care of her own problems.'

'That can happen.'

'It sure can. I was left to fend for myself, run wild. How do you think that made me feel?'

He was sitting bolt upright in the chair, his shoulders stiff and his face rigid.

'I imagine it made you feel unsafe. We all need to be nurtured. And when the time is right, we establish ourselves as independent, actualized people, but first we need that sense of security.'

'So you saying that I have to regress or something? Do some of that rebirthing shit?'

'I'm saying you need to reconcile yourself with that fear you're carrying, Alan – so bravely if I may say – from your past. You have coped and struggled in that coping. You need to give yourself a break. This is the time where you allow yourself to feel what was denied you in the past.'

'Well, who knows how that's going to turn out?' He paused, then looked straight at me. His body was still stiff and tensed, like he was ready to spring from the chair. 'Like I say, maybe I need a mother. Maybe that's why I never have any success in relationships because I'm looking for that person to fill the gap.'

'That's insightful of you.'

'Maybe you're that person.' He laughed after he said that, but his posture remained stiff.

I was used to transference, but this felt like something else. He was playing with the idea.

'Only messing with you,' he said eventually. 'Do you think I really want another mother? The first one I had was bad enough. Why would I want to repeat the experience?'

'We tend to repeat experiences until they enter our awareness.'

'Maybe there are some things I'd rather not be aware of. Unless you want to be my ma. Maybe you do. Maybe you'd get off on that.'

I didn't respond to that, instead let the silence settle. We stayed in silence for a couple of minutes. Alan looked wildly around the room.

'Well, I don't pay good money to sit here like some sort of arsehole, now, do I?'

'No, you don't. I was waiting for you to continue.'

'I think I'm done with that. It's time for you to give me some advice, don't you think? Isn't that what I pay you for?' He paused and added, 'Mummy,' then laughed too loud. His expression remained hard.

'What sort of advice were you hoping for?' I asked Alan.

He ran his fingers through his hair. 'You tell me. Isn't that what you're supposed to do?'

We parried back and forth for the rest of the session. He remained on edge throughout. I tried to bring the wild energy back down, but Alan resisted at every turn. When he left, he still looked agitated, his long limbs swinging loosely as he made his way out the door.

The session had left me feeling unnerved, but that was nothing new. Clients were often most agitated right before a breakthrough, and that was where I hoped Alan was at.

I walked to a local convenience store at lunchtime – to clear my head as well as to get the falafel wrap and freshly squeezed orange juice that I often bought. I took them to the park and settled on my usual bench, out of the view of prying eyes.

I thought about what Daniel had said to me about Pete. My first thought was, *What the hell was Pete doing, suddenly feeling the need to confess?* That annoyed me. Pete had been my friend too, and if he felt the need to confess now, surely he should have told me first. Putting that annoyance aside, I thought about how knowing about it must be hurting Daniel.

What I had said to him was true though. There had been so much stuff going on for me at the time, and I really hadn't been sure if I was a suitable partner for anyone. I had been going through personal counselling and exposed some raw truths about my survival at home. Yes, I had served the role of peacemaker, but had I just been covering up for my alcoholic father? He would often fly into drunken rages, and whoever got in his way was in for it. My mother had stood up to him, and she'd paid the price. What I had seen I'd tried to bury, but it was there all the time. I could still hear, smell, almost taste the feeling of helplessness as he tore into her. Revisiting all that made me feel so unprepared for a relationship, and well, maybe Pete took advantage of that, or maybe I was looking for an excuse to bail out.

I tried to distract myself before going back to work and tuned in to the familiar trilling of a blackbird overhead. I did a short grounding exercise that I have done so many times with clients, allowing myself to see, hear, feel and smell everything in the present. Then I made my way back to work, hoping the cloud of worry had evaporated and I would be able to give my clients the attention they deserved.

That aspiration didn't last too long. It disappeared as soon as I reached the side door that leads to the ground floor and my office. I fumbled in my bag and then my jacket pocket, but I couldn't find my keys.

I must have left them on my desk, I thought. But that thought was accompanied by the niggling certainty that I had never done that before.

I rang the bell, and after a long pause, the door upstairs was opened.

Dorothy shouted, 'Who is it?' She sounded irritable.

Like someone who has had their lunch interrupted, I thought.

I made my way around to the front and up the flight of stone steps to the ground floor where Dorothy's office was. The building was divided into upstairs downstairs. Where my office was had probably been the servants' quarters in grandiose times.

'Sorry about that,' I said briskly. 'I seem to have misplaced my keys. They're probably in my office.'

'I hope so,' Dorothy replied before disappearing back into her office.

But when I got down to my own spartan, tidy office, the keys were nowhere to be seen. I checked my pockets and my bag again and again, but they weren't there. There was nothing in the office they could be hidden under. Everything was straight lines and deliberately ordered. I tried to keep my office simple and uncluttered to help my clients focus.

I stood in the middle of the office and scanned it nonetheless, thinking my state of distraction might have been partly responsible for the loss. I kept my client files in a steel filing cabinet in the corner of the room and occasionally left the keys dangling in the lock as I went looking for a particular file, but they weren't there either. I checked around the communal kitchen and asked a few of my fellow counsellors if they'd seen them, but no joy.

That got me worried. All my keys were on that bunch, which meant house keys as well as those for work. I also had a spare car key on it, although I kept one in my bag too. At least I would be able to get home. However, there was no getting away from what I had to do next. I went upstairs and knocked softly on Dorothy's door. Standing there, feeling guilty, made me think of school days when you had to go into another classroom to get something. You had this momentary, irrational fear that anything could happen when the door swung open.

I heard Dorothy calling from inside. 'Yes?'

I pushed the heavy wooden door slowly open, feeling an involuntary shake weakening my arm strength. *This is ridiculous*, I thought. *She might be the boss of the place, but she's just a human being too.* With that thought bolstering me, I walked with some effort to stand in front of her desk.

'Dorothy, you know I told you I had lost my keys; well, I can't find them anywhere. I really have no clue where they might be. I've looked everywhere.'

Dorothy eyed me unsympathetically from the other side of her wide wooden desk. I could see remnants of her lunch scattered in front of her – an open greaseproof sandwich wrapper, a cardboard coffee cup, some sort of cereal bar wrapper beside the coffee cup.

'Were all the keys on that bunch, as in the keys to your entrance downstairs as well?' She regarded me over her gold-framed glasses and made me feel every inch the recalcitrant schoolgirl.

'Yes, I'm afraid so, but I'm sure they'll turn up. Actually, now that I think of it, I haven't checked the car yet.' I blurted that out but knew in my heart of hearts that they wouldn't be there. I only went to the car to sneak a quick smoke during the day, and my willpower had held out so far.

'Okay, well, you'd better get a move on, then, and check everywhere. Let me know if you find them.'

I went straight to the car and had the briefest of looks, but as I suspected, there was no sign of them. I did use the opportunity though to spark up a smoke and inhale deeply, feeling the nicotine creeping into every pore in my body, loving and hating the sensation at the same time, as I always did. Giving up smoking had become my personal Everest, something I would one day achieve or die trying.

Reluctantly, at the end of the working day, I had to put a call through to Dorothy and let her know the keys hadn't been found.

She sighed and said, 'Well, if they don't turn up, we're going to have to get the locks changed.' There was a pause, and then she said, 'Nicole, are you sure you're not too distracted to give your full attention to your work?'

'Yes, I'm sure,' I muttered, but my reassurance sounded weak and defensive.

'It might be a good time for you to take a break,' she continued. 'Sometimes we need to get away from routine and check in with ourselves. It's only then that we can see what's really going on.'

'I think I've spent enough time checking in with myself after that last incident. I need the purpose and focus of work.'

'But that doesn't seem to be working out so well for you, Nicole, does it?'

'I think it's working okay. There's going to be some little blips here and there.'

'Blips, Nicole? In our profession, do you think we can afford many blips?'

'There won't be any more,' I said with as much resolution as I could muster.

I left work not feeling very good about myself. I understood Dorothy's point of view, but at the same time, I didn't think she needed to be quite so harsh about it.

She was not only the boss but our counselling supervisor, the person we reported to when cases got tricky or if we just needed to offload. She had been a counsellor for years before she'd taken the step to open up her own business. I wondered if the move had dragged her into a place of responsibility that she found hard to handle. Still, she could be more sympathetic. We all made mistakes. I was also worried about the prospect that all my keys were out there somewhere. With all the weird stuff that had been going on, it was a most disconcerting feeling. I called a locksmith and made an appointment for both work and home, but it would be a couple of days before they got to me.

I had texted Daniel earlier to tell him about the key; he always had a spare just in case. I dropped by his place and picked it up on the way home. I was relieved to finally get into the house and reheat some pasta bake that I had made the day before. Pablo was due over at eight, and I was very much looking forward to his reassuring presence. I didn't think there was a connection between my lost keys and the other stuff that had been going on, but there remained a niggling doubt. What if someone had been following me and saw the opportunity to grab them? I had no doubt that someone was toying with me, so what a victory that would be if they managed to get hold of my keys. I would be a hostage to them until I got my locks changed.

I heard the doorbell ring. It was one of those old-style chimes that literally bing bongs around the hallway. I had never had it changed. Daniel and I had liked its old-world charm, so we'd left it in situ, sometimes even imitating the noise as we went to answer the door.

Not this time.

I walked with trepidation, glancing down the hallway, to see a figure in the frosted glass at the side of the door. The figure moved. They wore dark clothing and appeared to be shuffling restlessly. I was just about to shout and ask who it was when I heard a familiar voice.

'Nicole, let me in. Man, I need to pee bad.'

It was the husky tones of my own Pablo. I yanked the door open with relief and delight to see the poor guy hopping from foot to foot. That explained the shuffling. He darted past me and into the downstairs loo.

'Oh, man. I needed that. Drank too much water during class. Those classrooms, they're stuffy. Too many students. Boss wants to make a quick buck, so who am I? Just some dumbass teacher.'

He emerged from the loo and kissed me, then stood back and frowned. 'You look stress. What's wrong?'

I slipped an arm around his waist, glad to have the physical contact. It immediately made me feel grounded.

'I'm okay. Thanks for noticing. I lost my keys, and just with everything else, it got me freaked out. All my keys were on the bunch – work, home, the lot. It's going to be a couple of days before the locksmith is out to change the locks and give me new keys.

Pablo shook his head, then put his arms around me. 'It's okay. I'm here now. Listen, we get some takeaway. Ben coming over later, yeah? We make a nice night, just the three of us.'

That sounded so good to me I almost burst into tears. *My God, I must be really stressed,* I thought, *if something like that can set me off.*

'That would be lovely,' I said when the tearful moment had passed.

We already had an Indian takeaway sitting in brown bags on the table, oozing smells of cardamom, coriander, and cumin by the time Daniel dropped Ben over. The three of us sat down to watch repeats of *Father Ted*, which Ben had recently discovered, and stuffed our faces, slobbing out completely on the long, leather couch.

I put Ben to bed about ten and put the latch on the front door, so even if someone had a key, they couldn't get in. Then I ran a bath and went to bed. Pablo was staying up to do some Facebook catch-up.

I must have fallen into a deep sleep because I didn't notice him come to bed. I woke somewhere in the depths of the night and checked my phone to see what time it was. 4am.

I needed to pee, but I heard a noise, faint but persistent, coming from downstairs. I thought of waking Pablo, but my need to pee got the better of me, and I stumbled out to the bathroom. After, I paused and listened.

There it was again, something almost like a scratching at the front door. I turned on the landing light and went halfway down the stairs.

Click, click, click.

What was it? I walked a couple of steps farther down so I could see the front door.

Click, click, click.

It was a noise that was familiar to me, but at the same time unnerving.

Click, click, click.

Then a gust of wind blew outside, and the clicking came even faster. I laughed. It was the sound of the little knocker, just over the letterbox, the small steel knocker that sometimes got lifted by the wind.

I went back to bed, but sleep was proving elusive. Upon shutting my eyes, all I could hear was that clicking noise, although I wasn't sure the noise was even there anymore. The noise had been so persistent, had sounded too regular, too even to be the wind. But maybe that was my mind playing tricks.

I felt perspective slipping away. Was it possible someone was out there, and they'd stopped once the landing light went on? Then by coincidence a gust of wind had rattled it? Possible, yes, but very unlikely.

Still, once that thought had got a foothold in my mind, it wouldn't let go. I lay there listening. Sleep deserted me completely. I had become fixated on the noise, couldn't think of anything else, until dawn started bleeding through the curtains, and I finally got up.

10

DANIEL

I wondered how Nicole was after her experiences at work and the argument we'd had about Pete. I felt a bit guilty for bringing it up there and then, but as Pamela had said, maybe it was a good way of seeing Nicole's reaction, to get a sense of where she was in the real world. She'd been defensive, as anyone would expect, and she'd been apologetic. I guessed they were pretty normal reactions, but she had also mentioned the stress and confusion at the time of the affair. However, I didn't feel she was trying to cover anything up. My only question was, and I guess it was the big question: how in control of her thoughts and actions was she?

I'd had an okay day in work, selling a few bits and pieces to some passing trade and getting a good few online enquiries. Easter break was coming, and there was a sense in the air that better weather would be coming too, and maybe that had added an extra spring to the collective step of the shoppers.

I arrived home feeling more upbeat than I had been and gave Ben a quick kiss on his head as he slouched to eat some macaroni cheese that Pamela had cooked up.

'Daaad,' he said when I kissed him, giving me a mild irritated reaction. His eleventh birthday was coming up soon, so
I guessed those expressions of irritation might get pretty real
in a couple of years' time. I was determined to enjoy the last
of the boyhood years while I could.

Pamela went out to her evening classes at seven, and that
left me and Ben alone. I helped him with his homework,
trying desperately to remember how to do long division so I
could make it look easy for him. I was wary of tripping myself
up with carrying numbers all over the place.

Finally, we got the maths homework done, and he got a
few gap-fill English vocab exercises done too, so we were able
to sit back and watch the quiz show *The Chase*. Ben wasn't
really into sports, but he did shine at general knowledge and
had a flair for the Rubik's Cube as well. Both things might get
him labelled 'nerdy', but he didn't seem to care. Neither did I.

I made him a hot chocolate and was watching him take
tentative sips of the hot liquid when he turned to me.

'Dad,' he said, his puzzled look throwing lines across his
forehead.

'Yes?'

'I couldn't sleep very well last night.'

'Oh, why not?'

'I don't know, but I got up late, and I was looking out my
door into the main room. Pablo was there. Mum had gone to
bed.'

'Yes?' I was beginning to feel a knot of tension twisting in
my stomach. I felt whatever he said next was probably not
going to be good.

'Well, you know the way you said I should, like, spy on
Mam and what's going on in the house?'

'I didn't say spy. I said just keep an eye on things and let
me know if there's anything that bothers you.'

'Yeah, well, this may be one of those things.'

'Oh? Tell me.'

'I heard Pablo talking on the phone. He was speaking in Spanish, but I know enough Spanish now. I've been doing it a lot.'

'What was he saying?'

'I didn't understand everything, but I understood enough. He said something about the plan going well.'

'The plan?'

'Yeah, something about a plan.'

'Oh, but I suppose that could be anything.'

'He was whispering into the phone.'

'Yes, but it was late at night.' I was making excuses for Pablo, but there could be a reasonable explanation. And he probably didn't want to wake anyone.

'Pablo doesn't normally talk quietly. He has this loud Spanish voice.' Ben paused then and wrinkled his nose. 'Do all Spanish people talk loud?'

I laughed, glad at the opportunity to find some levity. 'Well, maybe the question there is do all Irish people talk quietly? It's a different culture, isn't it?'

'Do we talk quietly? The principal in our school doesn't talk quietly. If she sees you running in the corridor, she shouts at you to stop.'

'That's principals for you. Tough job controlling all those kids. Now, don't you worry about whatever Pablo was saying. I'm sure it's nothing, but thanks for telling me.'

Ben went to bed shortly after. Pamela came home, but I had made a decision not to say anything to her about what Ben had said. I'd wait and talk to Nicole first. I felt Pamela was already looking unfavourably upon Nicole because of the thing with Pete.

I got a chance to talk to Nicole the next day. I phoned her during her lunchbreak, and she picked up straight away.

'Yes?' Nicole didn't sound too friendly. There was obviously a bit of tension left over from our discussion about Pete.

'Hi, listen, hope everything is okay with you now, but there is something I need to tell you. It might or might not be important, but with all the stuff going on, I thought you should know.'

'What is it?' Nicole's tone was urgent.

'It's to do with Pablo. Ben was up late the other night. He couldn't sleep.'

'And?'

'Well, he said he was looking out his bedroom door into the living room, and Pablo was on the phone to someone. He was speaking in Spanish.'

'Yes, and? He is Spanish, for God's sake.'

I could hear impatience in her voice now, but I didn't want to rush or sensationalize the news. 'It's just that, you know Ben has been studying Spanish, so he's picked up a bit. He said he heard Pablo say something about a plan.'

'A plan?'

'Yeah. He said the plan was going well. Now, that's all Ben heard or was able to understand.'

'But that could have been anything – I mean the plan.'

'Yes, that's what I said to Ben, but just because of the weird stuff that's been happening, I thought you should know.'

'I don't know what to say, Daniel. I suppose I should say thanks for telling me, but I'm sure it's absolutely nothing.'

'I'm sure it is too. He seems like a good guy. I just thought you should know.'

We left the conversation there, and although I felt like a bit of a drama queen, I would have been kicking myself if I hadn't told her and then it did turn out to be something serious. Nicole needed to know what was going on around her.

Then she could make her own judgement about how she should react.

Ben was staying with me again that night, so I set about reassuring him that everything was fine with Pablo and that he had nothing to worry about. Nicole and I had spoken about it, and the whole thing was sorted.

'So it was good of you to tell me what you heard, but you can relax now. You just make sure you get a good night's sleep when you're over there and leave all the other stuff to the adults.'

He nodded in agreement at that, and I gave him a hug. Sometimes he was just too sweet for words.

11

NICOLE

What Daniel had said about Pablo was worrying. It bothered me on a couple of fronts.

One, the most obvious, was that Pablo was hiding something from me. The other was that Ben felt the need to report back to Daniel and not me. It was like I was being watched in my own home, that the people I loved were uncertain about my state of health. I'd done enough introspection on that myself. I didn't need anyone else doing it as well.

So I thought about it during the afternoon. I had to admit, I didn't know a whole lot about Pablo's background, but in a way that absolutely suited me. I didn't want anything too serious after what had happened with Daniel. Pablo and I got along. We fancied each other in a giddy, almost adolescent way, and we got each other's sense of humour, and that was plenty to be going on with for now. He got on well with Ben as well, and they had the Spanish language thing going on. I had been slow to introduce him to Ben, but they had got along so well from the start that I had lost my initial reticence. But now I had to contend with the fact that I didn't truly know him that well. I had to think about how to approach this new piece of information.

I was in Spanish class that night, and as usual, the vibes between Pablo and me had a nice little current of electricity. Covert glances and smiles and answers to questions that involved lengthy eye contact. I looked at him – slim, brown-skinned, warm-eyed, smiling – and saw nothing whatsoever that could be construed as sinister. We had sushi afterwards and half a bottle of saki before walking home with a warm afterglow. After, we sank into bed together.

Pablo was tired, so he stayed on in bed, but I still had a little restlessness to contend with after the saki wore off. So I stayed up flicking around the stations, absorbing bits of trash along with news repeats, until I grew weary of both. Looking around the room in search of distraction, my eyes landed on Pablo's laptop. I had a quick look into the bedroom and saw he was fast asleep, snoring deeply in that way that made me jealous during my fitful sleeps.

Feeling a little guilty and moving with the stiff awkward-ness that often accompanies guilt, I flipped his laptop open and went straight to Facebook. I knew he spent time on that late at night, catching up with friends. I guessed if there was anywhere the new information could be confirmed or denied, it would probably be there.

His password was saved, so it was just a case of clicking in. There in front of me were various postings, what you would expect from a man-about-town in his thirties – music, foot-ball, more music, newly discovered IPAs, shared videos of stupid stuff, cat-stuck-in-the-trash-can type of thing, some sexy shots of straight-up raunchy women and so on. It all looked very Iberian and colourful to my Irish eyes that were used to a greyer pallet. So nothing out of the ordinary there.

I paused before thinking about clicking on his private messages. That was taking the snooping a step further, but I vowed to myself that if I did it and found nothing, then that was the end. I would never snoop again.

With a justification for my actions, I clicked on the messages. The immediate problem was, of course, that I had limited Spanish. What I could make out looked like casual banter along the lines of 'what you up to' and 'miss you' and 'want to have beers soon'. Nothing strange in what I could make out, but what was strange was that Pablo's name was never used. Instead they seemed to be calling him Juan. I wasn't sure if it was my poor understanding of the language and context, but it definitely looked like he was being referred to as Juan. It came up in a few messages from different people. I snapped the laptop shut and put it back where I'd found it.

My heart was pounding. I wasn't sure what I was going to do. Could I ask him directly? I'd have to admit that I had been snooping, and that was a breach of trust. But then, if he was operating under some sort of dual identity, that was definitely something I needed an answer to. I decided to sleep on it and see what I came up with the next day. Sleep, naturally, didn't come easy after that, but I managed to get a few hours and hoped that once I got into work mode, I'd get a fresh boost of energy.

That didn't prove to be the case.

I had still been looking for my keys, hoping that they would turn up somewhere, thinking maybe someone would find them in some obscure part of the building or mixed up in the gravel of the car park, but no, they hadn't been found. I was still waiting for the locksmith to put new locks in. But when I got in that morning and walked into my office, I realised somebody had already been there.

The wooden clock on the mantelpiece, the heirloom from my grandparents' house, was no longer there. It was missing, and all that was left was the faint trace of an outline on the wallpaper against which it had stood. That clock had never once been moved in all the time I had been here. It was a grounding point for both me and my clients, and now it was gone.

I didn't know how to react, but I had a sickly feeling in my stomach that threatened to overwhelm me. There was no doubt that someone had moved or possibly taken it, and if I was to start asking questions, then Dorothy would know, and I would be responsible for a security breach. The only person who might have moved the clock – and it was a very slim chance – was Magda, the no-nonsense Polish cleaner. I waited until she appeared in the hallway and ushered her into my room, pointing at the space on the mantelpiece.

'Magda, did you take the clock to clean it, or were you dusting around the mantelpiece?'

'Clock?' she asked, looking bemused. She was in her late forties and had a girly bob of blonde hair that framed a wide, strong-featured face. 'No, didn't touch clock.' She shook her head to reinforce the message, shrugged her shoulders and left me alone to stare at the empty space.

Okay, so someone had come into the office and taken it. Did someone want to send me a message that my workspace was no longer safe?

My first client of the day arrived before I had time to figure out what to do. I found myself constantly looking to the mantelpiece and then having to look at the watch on my wrist to make sure I didn't go over time. It was all very disconcerting. I found it hard to concentrate. Who had taken the clock, and why did they take only the clock?

The answer spinning around my mind was that they

wanted me to know I was under their control, that they could toy with me. Just like the incident when I'd been working late. It had been a subtle, gradual buildup, first throwing pebbles at the window, then shining the torch in. It could have been anyone, could have been someone messing around, but no, when I had put everything together, there had been a pattern. Whoever it was wanted me to know they had me exactly where they wanted me. Now they had the keys to my house and to my place of work. The locks would be changed in the next day or two, but I still had to tell Dorothy I hadn't found the keys. No way was I telling her the clock had also gone missing.

I broached the subject with her at lunchtime. Dorothy always seemed to be sequestered in her office upstairs, various items of food scattered across her broad wooden desk. She didn't mix with the rest of us, something I put down to her dual role of boss and supervisor. She couldn't get too entangled in our personal stories, but part of me wondered if she just liked the solitude. Many of us counsellors carried our own burdens. The expression 'the wounded healer' was one I'd heard often when studying psychotherapy. Did Dorothy have her own wounds that she was trying to shield?

'So you can't find them. Well, that is problematic.' Dorothy hadn't gestured for me to sit, so I stood awkwardly in front of her desk while she scrutinized me. 'But you've arranged for a locksmith to come out. I'll still have to tell the other counsellors, and they won't be happy about it.' She let that sentence hang in the air.

'I'll pay for the new set of course,' I blurted out.

'That would be a help, I suppose.' Her tone softened.

'Okay,' I agreed, happy to have the matter settled. I started walking towards the door.

'Nicole,' Dorothy said languidly, 'you won't forget to follow through with the locksmith now, will you?'

'Of course not.'

But the remark stung as I made my way back downstairs again. Why did she have to throw that in at the end, like she was dealing with someone who couldn't remember to carry out the simplest of tasks? Did she think I had lost it to that extent?

I focused as much as I could for the afternoon, giving my clients the attention they deserved. But in the back of my mind was the interaction with Dorothy. She had spoken to me like I was someone who was incapable of performing the most menial tasks, like I was losing my mind. That undermined my confidence in myself, but I did my best to keep a positive, confident attitude with my clients.

And then there was Pablo. What was I going to do about him?

I gave it some thought on the way home. It wasn't something I could put off, not given the circumstances. I didn't really think that Pablo could be connected with the strange things that were happening, but could there be some connection? Could it even be something that he wasn't aware of? I had no idea what was going on, but if there was even the remotest chance my incidents had anything to do with him, I had to know.

Pablo and I sat down for some food at about seven. Ben was due over at eight. Time was of the essence. I had to level with him.

'Pablo, there's something I wanted to ask you about. It is personal, but I want to be direct with you because I trust you.'

He frowned and paused with a forkful of penne and pesto halfway to his mouth. 'Personal?' he asked.

'Yes, and I have to apologise at the same time because I looked at something I shouldn't have.'

The frown deepened. He regarded me warily. 'What you talking about, Nicole?'

'I was scrolling on your computer last night, you know, just looking around, and I logged in to Facebook. I thought it was my own account, but it was yours.' That lie slipped out easily. I felt terrible for saying it, but the prospect of telling him I had been deliberately looking into his account felt like an outrageous invasion of privacy.

'I saw messages to you, and I noticed that they weren't using your name. They were calling you Juan.'

Pablo put his forkful of food down. He was shaking his head. 'You shouldn't do that, Nicole. You shouldn't be looking in my Facebook.'

I reached across to hold his hand, but he pulled it away.

'I'm sorry, I really am, but there's been so much weird stuff happening. I'm scared. And when I saw that, it just set off alarm bells.'

'But that's my private account.'

I couldn't bring Ben into the conversation and how he had heard Pablo talking about a plan. I just couldn't. I had to take the rap for whatever consequences.

'I know it is, and I know I shouldn't have, but you know that I am scared at the moment, and I've told you about what happened before. I guess I am very watchful and very wary at the moment. I need things to be clear; otherwise I start to feel panicky. I just can't go down that road again.'

Pablo looked at me for what felt like a long time. I didn't see anger in his deep, brown eyes, but I saw scrutiny. Eventually he dropped his gaze to his plate.

'What you did, Nicole, you break the trust between us. You are scared, sure. Maybe I am scared too? Did you ever think of that? Maybe there is something that I need to be very scared of, but I haven't told you because I want to protect you.'

That made me sit back in my chair and look closely at him. 'If there is something like that, then you need to tell me.'

'I can't, not yet. I can only tell you when the time is right.'

'But Pablo, what am I supposed to think? What am I supposed to do?'

'Nothing. For you to do nothing is safest for now.'

12

DANIEL

I really hadn't been sure how to approach Nicole over the thing with Pablo, but lingering doubts plagued me all day at work. Was he connected to the strange stuff that was going on? Why did he have what he referred to as a plan, and more importantly, why did he feel the need to keep it secret?

I made a decision after a long day thinking about it. I was going to have to get close to Pablo, to try to sound him out, to see if he was a threat to Nicole and Ben. That was my main concern. I still couldn't be sure about Nicole's capacity for judgement. The incidents with James next door and her belief she was being framed, the mysterious person outside her workplace – how much of it had been real and how much fantasy?

In a way I wanted to believe that she was in full control of her mind and her emotions, but if so, that meant someone was really out to get her. Could that happen again? Was it Gary playing us off each other again? I didn't want to believe that she could be under attack again so soon after the last time. But it was either that or she was losing her mind. I had to do what I could to find out, so I put the first part of my plan into action that night.

Pamela had no classes, but she had a little writing to do. She finished up around eight. I had busied myself throwing a beef stir-fry together and cracked open a Cotes Du Rhone. When Pamela was seated, I poured her a glass, with the exaggerated mannerisms of a wine waiter. One arm behind my back, I tipped the bottle with a demonstrable grace so a thin stream of red wine dropped neatly into her glass. She gave me a playful shove when I had finished.

'Messer,' she said with a laugh.

'*Monsieur*, you surely mean, *Madame*?'

'No, messer.' She dug her fork into the tangle of noodles and shredded beef. 'Looks tasty.'

She lifted a large portion off her plate. 'God, who would have thought there'd be so much company law in HR?'

'The underwriters perhaps?'

Pamela let out a chortle. 'Apart from them.'

'Well, my dear, they are omnipresent in the world of business. And this is the age of libel, so they'll only get busier, I suppose.'

'Box ticking is what it is. But why do we have to actually learn company law? Surely a quick Google search would do.'

'You have to at least have the appearance of being in control. Don't worry, you'll probably never use it. Just learn the stuff and be done with it.'

We devoured our food and wine, and after, I broached the subject I had been thinking about.

'Listen, you know the way things have been a little difficult between myself and Nicole, what with the Pete thing and then the stuff going on with the neighbour... Well, I was thinking it might be nice to have a bit of a meetup with Nicole and Pablo, to normalize things.'

'Don't let me stop you.'

'Well, you have a part to play as well. I thought it would be nice for the four of us to head out to dinner together. We've never really acknowledged Pablo, and he does look like he's in for the long haul.'

'Dinner? But what'll we talk about? I haven't even met him yet.'

'Exactly. It would be a good way to meet him, on neutral territory, just the four of us. We can go to that cute little Italian in town and quaff a bit of Chianti, loosen things up a bit.'

'Hmm, maybe, if you say so. I'd go more for you though than for Nicole or Pablo.'

'I don't mind who you go for as long as you go.' I smiled. 'You can dazzle them with your in-depth knowledge of company law.'

I put the plan straight into action by texting Nicole and arranging it for the following night. I would get a babysitter for Ben. I also insisted on paying for the dinner, as I had made a good few sales. That last bit was stretching the truth. There had been a few sales, but business was still sluggish.

Anyway, Nicole agreed. It was a Friday, so Pablo had no class, and Nicole agreed it would be nice for us all to meet up.

We met in the small Italian that Nicole and I had frequented during our courting days. It had an old-school, almost musty smell, as if you were genuinely walking into someone's living room. Just a few tables scattered around the place, dark-stained wood floor, and curtains covering the windows blocking the view of the city outside. It had recreated the feeling one got when stepping off the busy streets of modern life and into a time capsule, where you were guaranteed attention and a chance to slow down.

Pablo ran an approving eye over the place, nodding and saying, 'Is nice.'

He looked smart in his brown, corduroy sports jacket and

light-green flannel shirt. He and Nicole sat hunched together over the menu, which was sparse on choice and to the point, written out in italics to make it look handwritten.

Pamela had put her menu down and was observing the pair. 'You're probably used to this type of food,' she said to Pablo, who looked up from the menu.

'A little, but I am Spanish.'

'Yes, but Mediterranean food. All pretty similar.'

'Maybe, but we have our traditional dishes like paella that they don't have in Italy.'

'But they like fish and seafood as well in Italy, don't they?' For some reason she turned to me with that question.

'Oh, so I'm the resident expert on Italian food now, am I?' I asked with a smile. 'My ego, it's taking off.'

Pamela frowned. 'Don't be silly. I was just checking. It's not like I get out much between work and college.' She went back to studying her menu, and I was left wondering what the comment about not getting out much meant.

'How's the shop?' Nicole asked me.

'Okay, ticking over.'

'I thought you said you had sold a good bit,' Pamela said.

Ooops, I thought, *I did say that as a pretext for inviting everyone out.*

'Yes, well, it was relatively good, I suppose.' I felt that was a suitable fobbing off, then turned to Pablo to change the conversation. I had come here with a purpose, and I was going to see it through.

'How is the Spanish teaching going? That must be hard. Teaching an entire language can't be easy.'

Pablo smiled and looked at Nicole. There was genuine warmth between them. I was happy to see that warmth, even if it did make me sad that my ex and I had lost that same warmth somewhere along the way.

'This is one of my best students right here beside me.'

'One of your best students?' Nicole asked in a deliberately high-pitched voice. 'Only one of your best? Not *the* best?'

Pablo laughed. 'Of course you are, but I didn't want to embarrass you.' He leaned over and kissed her.

'It must take a lot of training to be able to teach like that.'

'Of course, yes. University degree and then teaching qualification.'

'Probably any degree, or did you have to do a specific one?'

I thought I saw Pablo flinch when I asked that. I realised I was verging on the edge of prying, but I didn't care. I was going to see what reaction I got.

'Yeah, like an arts degree, as you call it here,' Pablo answered.

'Interesting. A good foundation for education they say is the arts degree. Pamela would know that, being in HR now... well, almost in HR.'

'Thanks for the almost,' Pamela said humourlessly.

I tried to rub her shoulder, but she pulled away. 'Pamela is studying HR, and the company law bit is driving her mad.'

'It would drive anyone mad, I'm sure,' Nicole said.

'You didn't study law, did you, Pablo?' I asked. 'Maybe you could help Pamela out.'

'No, just general arts, like I said,' he replied.

'Oh, so it's like the American system, then,' I persisted. 'General degree and then a master's afterwards.'

Nicole looked up sharply at me. 'Why all the questions? Are you thinking of going into HR yourself?'

I laughed, even though Nicole's tone had been serious. 'Not a bad idea. No, I'm just curious about other cultures, I suppose.'

'That's a trait I hadn't noticed before,' Nicole said sardonically.

The *primi piatti* arrived and provided some distraction

from the tension. Pablo was uneasy, and that was exactly how I wanted him.

'*Parmegianno?*' the waiter asked, a man whom I had just heard speaking in a strong Dublin accent. He reverted to a full-blown Italian accent as he produced a wooden parmesan dispenser, which he offered to everyone in turn.

'Shall we get a second bottle?' Pamela was tipping the last of the first bottle into her glass. I saw her cheeks were already a little flushed. She sometimes drank a bit too quickly if she was anxious or uptight. I thought maybe my questioning of Pablo was adding to that, so I decided to hold back a little. I signaled to the waiter for another bottle.

We chitchatted a little, discussed the merits of *zuppa minestrone* versus *bruschetta* and drank more Chianti before I decided enough of a lull had passed for me to resume my interrogation of Pablo.

'What's employment like in Spain at the moment?'

'Depends on the work, you know, a lot of tourism work in Spain.'

I was just formulating my next question when Pamela jumped in.

'So it's better for you to be here,' she said.

'Yes, of course.'

'In a country that's not your own.'

Pablo looked at Pamela like he was trying to figure out her meaning. He said nothing.

'We need Spanish teachers,' I said quickly. 'I bet Nicole would agree with that.'

Nicole laughed and rubbed Pablo's shoulder, but Pamela wasn't finished. I could see her cheeks had reddened considerably from the wine.

'I'm sure there's plenty of people here who would like the opportunity to be Spanish teachers. We need to give our own a chance.'

'What do you mean by that?' Nicole asked sharply. A knot of tension formed in my stomach.

'Just what I said. I'm sure there are plenty of jobs where Pablo comes from.' Pamela took a large swig of her wine.

'I don't agree,' I said quickly. 'It's a different world we live in now, more of an international community, isn't it? The labour market is very fluid these days, and that's a good thing as far as I'm concerned.'

'I agree,' Nicole said. 'I think it's good to learn from a native speaker, and I think it's good to have a mix of cultures.' Her eyes zeroed in on Pamela. 'Maybe you should have travelled a bit more yourself.'

'Listen, we forget about it, okay?' Pablo said, putting a hand on Nicole's, which was on the table. 'People say things sometimes. They don't mean nothing bad.'

Nicole glared at Pamela, but she said nothing. The main course arrived, and we ate amid an uneasy silence that I tried to break with comments about the quality of the food. But the night was toast, and we were all glad to get out of there.

It hadn't been a good night, but my main regret was that I had got nowhere close to unsettling Pablo so he might reveal something of what his 'plan' was.

13

NICOLE

The night out with Daniel and Pamela had been a disaster. Pablo had been upset by it, but he told me on Saturday morning, before he left for work, that he'd tell me what the thing with the name change was about later on.

'Pamela, she's not so nice a person. Maybe she got her own problems,' he had said last night. I felt he was being diplomatic because Daniel hadn't been too nice either.

In the meantime, I had Ben for the weekend. I had something else on my mind as well – I was seeing Alan for another session on Monday. I wondered if he was finally going to tell me his secret.

I took Ben to the zoo on Saturday afternoon for some much-needed distraction. We watched a colony of chimps going about their business on an island set in the middle of a big pond. Their comings and goings were largely harmonious, but every now and then there would be a shriek, or a scream of rage would erupt, and we'd see one of the group members being chased away. Order would then resume until the next outburst. It looked like a well-ordered society, governed by the issuing of immediate consequences for rule-breakers.

It made me think of the complexity of our own society and how, as a counsellor, I spent so much time trying to weave people back into the social fabric. Alan was one such person, looking like a success story from the outside but feeling completely disconnected on the inside, incapable of forming the relationships he wanted because of past experience.

I was thinking that and looking distractedly at the chimps when I looked down to say something to Ben and saw an empty space where he had been standing. There was quite a crowd around me, everyone laughing at the chimps' antics, so it took me some time to check through the throng for Ben. I couldn't see him anywhere. I had been distracted by the chimps for a few minutes, so I couldn't be sure how long ago he had wandered off.

Panic started to set in, but I took a few deep breaths and reassured myself. Ben was ten years old. He was a bit spacey, but he was a savvy enough kid. He probably got bored and wandered off to look at something else. I passed small crowds of people staring at the tigers, at the penguins, at the seals getting fed, but still no sign of my son.

The zoo suddenly looked like a frightening and alien place, full of squawking, squealing, roaring animals and people who were bustling in small, excited bunches from place to place. As I scanned the crowds frantically, there was a sense of chaos about the place despite its bars and enclosures. It felt like anything could happen there at any moment. I tried to remind myself that it was actually a safe place, that the people who designed zoos put an absolute premium on safety – with so many kids they had to. But after what had recently happened to me, that sense of safety was lost.

I saw just a vacuum, a space where Ben could disappear

or be taken. Whoever was targeting me could as easily target Ben. Look what had happened with Gary – he had turned on Daniel when he couldn't get to me.

I decided to go to security and report him missing. He had only been gone a few minutes, but there was an empty hollow at my core. I found it hard to even swallow, and I wasn't sure if I'd be able to speak to explain what had happened. I was approaching the main entrance, which was where I figured the security office would be, when I saw a familiar blue jacket and a brown bob of wavy hair moving ahead of me on the path.

'Ben,' I shouted. There was a fresh wind blowing, so he didn't hear me. I started running after him. He was walking quickly towards the entrance.

'Ben,' I shouted again, this time louder. Groups of people coming in looked over at me.

Thankfully, he stopped and turned around. He glanced back towards the entrance, but stood still and waited. I rushed up to him and threw my arms around him.

'Ben, where are you going? What are you doing?'

'I was going after somebody. They lost their money. They dropped it beside me when we were watching the chimps. I wanted to give it back, but they didn't hear me. They've just gone out. I was following them.'

He looked desperately towards the entrance. In his hand he had a little see-through plastic bag with a ten-euro note and some change in it.

I took it off him and stared at it, trying to make sense of what he was telling me.

'It's a lot of money,' he explained. 'I wanted to give it back, but they were walking away too fast.'

'Why didn't you tell me? Who was it?'

'You were watching the monkeys, and I thought I'd catch them quickly, but I didn't.'

'That's very good of you,' I said, rubbing his hair, but the hollow feeling in my stomach had expanded. 'Let's walk to the entrance and see if you can spot the person.'

A feeling of dread flooded through me. I had a bad feeling that I wouldn't want to see this person, but I had to know. I had to know if something sinister was going on. Deep down, I prayed it was a mistake that Ben had found this bag of money.

There was a small exit gate beside the entrance. I explained to the guy who was manning it that we just needed to slip out for a second. Someone had dropped money, but we'd be right back.

Holding Ben's hand securely, I walked out to the open, tarmac space just outside the zoo proper. Across to the left and directly in front were open, green spaces and then farther down, to the right, was a large car park. There was a steady mill of people still coming in the entrance to the zoo.

'Do you see the person anywhere?' I asked.

Ben scanned the area, tilting his head this way and that so he could see around the crowds.

'There,' he said suddenly. 'Over there.' He pointed towards the car park.

'What did they look like?'

'It was hard to see. I only really saw them from the back, and they were dressed in, like, a long coat and hat.'

'A man or a woman?'

'I think it was a woman,' he said, scratching his head and looking puzzled. 'But they were very tall. Maybe it was a man. I'm not sure. They had dark jeans and trainers on though.'

I held his hand, and we hurried towards the car park. It took us a couple of minutes to get there. Cars were rolling out in a steady stream. Ben's forehead was wrinkled with concentration as he scanned the area.

'I don't see them. They must have got into a car,' he said.

I watched the procession of cars roll out. There were two exits, so the person could have used either one. If they saw us standing there and they wanted to avoid us, it would have been easy to escape. We waited a couple of minutes more, but Ben kept shaking his head. I figured he'd had enough, so I led him back to the zoo.

'We can leave the money in the office,' he said excitedly. 'That's what we do when we find money in school.'

'Good idea,' I agreed, even though I had a strong feeling nobody would come looking for it.

For the rest of the afternoon, I tried to concentrate on what we were looking at and sharing in Ben's enthusiasm. He forgot about the money as soon as we'd handed it in, but Ben finding it at all stayed with me for the day. I couldn't banish the thoughts of a person in dark clothing targeting my son. Who had it been, and what had they wanted? Could it have simply been an accident that the money had been dropped and then a coincidence that the person had left quickly?

I doubted it.

If not, had it been the person who was stalking me? I didn't have to think too long about that, but I did have to think more about what they were hoping to do. What if Ben had followed them all the way out? I couldn't let myself think about that.

Going home that evening, I was nervous. What if the person, whoever it was, had seen me leave the house and followed us to the zoo? Would the same person be waiting for us when we got back? The door locks still hadn't been changed since I lost the keys. The locksmith was due out to my house and to work on Tuesday.

I tried to look as confident and nonchalant as I could as I pulled into my short drive. Ben tumbled from the car and ran to the front door.

I gave a quick glance up and down the street, but everything was quiet. With a trepidation that I tried to mask in front of Ben, I opened the front door and walked tentatively into the hall, where I stopped to listen.

No sound, just the whirr and gentle rattle of the fridge. Ben was about to charge upstairs to his bedroom, probably to get on his computer, when I instinctively reached a hand out to stop him.

'Just a second, love. I think I left some windows open. It might be cold up there.'

He looked quizzically at me, but I ignored him and marched up the stairs, then quickly checked each of the rooms. Nothing.

'It's okay, love,' I shouted down. 'I didn't leave them open, and it's nice and warm after all.'

That night I was so glad to see Pablo arrive. I said nothing about my day until Ben had gone to bed, and even then I kept it to a minimum. I could see Pablo was looking more stressed than usual, and I knew he wanted to get everything off his chest.

But first, he said, 'That's scary,' when I told him about Ben nearly leaving the zoo. 'Weird. Who was it? Maybe just an accident. Listen, I got to tell you, you know about what I was saying the other day.'

I put my finger to my lips and turned up the volume on the TV. I didn't want Ben hearing anything he shouldn't. Pablo looked a little confused, so I mouthed *Ben*. He nodded, then spoke in a low voice.

'There are some things I didn't want to tell you, Nicole, not because I didn't trust you, but because I love you. I was afraid you would see me in a different way and then be scared off.'

'Okay, what is it?'

'So you saw they call me Juan on Facebook. Well, that is

my real name. I am Juan. I took the name Pablo because I had to change my identity.'

He waited a moment for that information to sink in. I wasn't sure how to react. This made sense. I had known him by a different name.

'The other thing I should tell you is that I am not Spanish. I am from Guatemala.'

'Oh,' I heard myself say in surprise. I wasn't sure what he was going to tell me next, but I felt myself tense up, ready for whatever was to come.

'I told you I had to talk to someone before I said what I need to say. That person is my brother. He's in trouble. It's because of him that I had to change everything.'

Pablo was sitting beside me on the couch. He was looking right into my eyes as he spoke. He held both of my hands in his. I could feel the warmth of his touch, and it gave me some comfort, but I really didn't know where this story was going. I took some consolation from the eye contact though. There was sincerity there, and what I sensed was vulnerability.

Pablo sighed, then took a deep breath before he spoke again. 'Okay, maybe you don't know so much about Guatemala, but it can be a dangerous place. Lots of drug business. My brother got caught up as many young men do. Then he messed up like a lot of young men do too. He spent money that wasn't his, thinking he could pay it back later, but for them there is no later. It is now or never. He had to run. So when someone runs, they turn on the family. We had to run too.'

'That's terrible,' I said, but the information was still sinking in too slowly. Everything I had thought about Pablo was being turned on its head.

'So that's how I end up here. And that's why I had to change my name. I needed a new identity.'

'You changed your name, or you got a whole new identity?'

'A whole new identity. It's the only way. They have their connections everywhere. I have Spanish ID now. You can do these things if you know the right people.'

I sat back on the couch and tried to process what he was saying. I glanced at the stairs again to make sure there was no sign of Ben. This was a whole other world I was being told about, one that I only knew from TV programmes.

'That's why I am afraid, Nicole. I have to hide my real identity for the moment. The time will pass, and I will be safe, but for now it is too risky.'

I lay in bed that night beside Pablo wondering if I really knew the person next to me. So many things of what I had learned I really liked. He was one of the sincerest people I had ever met.

But now I had to come to terms with the fact that there was a whole other side to him. A secret identity.

14

DANIEL

I felt bad about my behaviour in the restaurant on Friday, but it had been an opportunity to press Pablo and see how he reacted to my questions. When I went to collect Ben on the Sunday afternoon, that perspective changed. Nicole brought me into the house. She looked worried. Ben was upstairs playing on his computer. Nicole and I sat in the kitchen, and she slid a mug of tea over to me.

'I'm sorry about the other night,' I said. 'I was testing Pablo, to see how he would react under pressure. It's just... what's going on worries me. I want to keep you and Ben safe.'

Nicole shook her head. 'Forget about the other night. It wasn't pleasant, and I felt Pamela was way out of order, but it doesn't matter now. I have something to tell you, and you need to listen carefully. It will help clear things up about Pablo. But first I have to tell you about something else weird and unsettling that happened yesterday when I took Ben to the zoo.'

Nicole looked strained, with worry lines creasing at the corners of her eyes.

'What happened?'

'This is going to sound very weird, but then everything that's been happening has been weird. Someone appeared to deliberately drop a bag of money beside Ben, and then, when he went to give it back, they kept walking away, like they were trying to lead him somewhere. I caught up with him at the zoo entrance.'

Daniel couldn't believe it. 'You think they were trying to lure him out?'

'What else? I can't think of another reason.'

'Unless it was just a coincidence, and they were hurrying off.'

'Another coincidence? Daniel, I'm nervous, and now I'm not just nervous for me.'

'But who can it be doing this? Gary Mulligan? Again? Who knew you were going to the zoo?'

'Well, you and Pablo. Nobody else, really.'

I nodded and took that information in. Pablo was the only one besides me who had known Nicole's whereabouts unless Ben had told friends. But even if he had, that was hardly a reason to point fingers at either of them.

'It's not Pablo,' Nicole blurted, as if she'd read my mind. 'It couldn't be. Why would he?'

'I don't know, and I'm not trying to imply anything either way, but that stuff about the plan, what was that all about?'

'Me and Pablo had a chat about that. We're going to work on it together.'

'What do you mean? I think I need to know as well. This is a matter of safety for you and Ben.'

'There's stuff going on in Pablo's life. It's very difficult.'

'Yes, but I still need to know even if it is difficult.'

Nicole looked at the table for a while before lifting her head.

'Okay, I'll tell you what I know,' she said, 'but you have to promise to keep it to yourself.'

'You've got my word on that.'

Nicole took a deep breath and explained. 'Pablo isn't his real name, alright? His name is Juan. He's also not Spanish. He's from Guatemala.'

'Wow, that's quite a bit to take in, isn't it?'

'Yes, and there's more... well, the reason he had to do all of that. It's his brother, he got into the drugs, and then he blew a load of money belonging to the gang. They were after him, and he disappeared, so Pablo and his family had to disappear too.'

'Drugs gang?' I could hear the words echo in my head. This was taking a direction I was uncomfortable with.

'He took on a new identity, and that's where the name Pablo came from. He is registered as Spanish now.'

'So he has illegal documents?'

'He has what he needs to survive. It's hard for us to understand, but I Googled Guatemala, and it does have a serious problem with gangs. Pablo has been nothing but an honourable man. We have to give him a chance.'

'But what about you? What about Ben? If there are people after him, then it's just not safe.'

'He assures me that nobody knows where he is.'

'Except whoever he's in contact with on Facebook, and that could be anyone.'

'He's being super careful. He has to be, and he's been in Europe now for three years without any problems.'

I really didn't like what I was hearing. 'After what we've been through, we really don't need this, Nicole. All the strange stuff that's been happening to you. It could be connected. You just don't know.'

'I think I do know. If the people who are looking for Pablo find him, they won't be doing things like shining torches in my window at work. Anyway, they are looking for him not me, and that's if they are even looking for him. They're probably waiting for him to return to Guatemala.' Nicole sighed. 'I really like Pablo. Ben likes him too. He's a good guy, trust me.'

I wanted to trust Nicole, but I couldn't leave Ben exposed to a family feud with a drugs gang. It was one thing for her to take risks, quite another to put him at risk. I couldn't stop Nicole from seeing Pablo, but I could do some snooping of my own, see if he was up to anything we didn't know about.

I left with Ben shortly after, and on the drive home, I made my mind up that I was going to do some surveillance. I knew where Pablo worked. It was the school where Nicole did her Spanish classes. I knew roughly the times that he worked. There wasn't a whole lot more I knew about the guy, but a bit of watching might reveal a lot. If I found any clues that his story wasn't true, then maybe I would have concrete evidence to present to Nicole.

I felt too impotent as a bystander. I had to do something. I had to protect Ben and Nicole.

15

NICOLE

I had an uneasy, sleepless night, checking the doors and windows, and listening out for any unusual sounds. I was on my own in the house. Pablo had asked to stay, but I said I needed time to absorb what he had told me. That bit was true. I would have liked the security of his presence, but I needed time apart from him.

I did my best to get a few hours' sleep. I'd even sprinkled a little lavender oil on my pillow, had a hot bath and did a little yoga before going to bed. Every time I woke, the scene in the zoo would play over and over in my mind. Was the incident there connected to whatever else was going on? It could just have been a coincidence, but the sequence of events had set alarm bells ringing. There had been a sinister feel to the act. If it was connected, then someone was targeting Ben as well as me. And that brought the threat to a whole new level.

Then the thing with Pablo, what was I supposed to think? He'd spoken genuinely, yet had been living this lie while seeing me. Not telling me was, he'd said, for his own protection – probably for my protection too – but what was I to make of it all? I needed time, and more importantly, I needed to be in the right frame of mind for my clients in the morning. Alan was due back in. Was this going to be the session where he told me his secret?

From the moment Alan walked into my counselling room, he seemed different. Gone was the well-crafted bonhomie that he usually presented. He looked cowed and also angry. He threw himself in the chair opposite and stared at me in a challenging manner. Alan was a big guy, well over six feet, so to have someone like that sit opposite me and exude menace was quite unnerving. It wasn't the first time it had happened to me during a practice session, so I did what I knew to do. I took a couple of deep breaths and calmed down.

'How have you been since our last session?' I asked Alan.

'Not good.' He left the sentence hanging, as if to say, '*If you want to get more out of me, you're going to have to work for it.*'

'In what way?'

'In every way. I'm thinking what's the point of coming here at all.'

'Well, it might surprise you to hear that its quite a common reaction to counselling. A lot of stuff comes up, and our reaction is sometimes to run away from it. It's not pleasant, so why would we not have that reaction?'

'So what are you saying, then?' His facial expression was rigid, almost like someone had done a plaster cast of his face and he'd stuck it on.

'I'm just saying it's a normal part of the process.'

Alan kept staring at me. 'Well, maybe I found something out that makes it not quite so normal anymore.'

'Oh, is that something you want to tell me about?'

'I'll tell you when I'm ready and when I feel safe. Maybe sometime when this place is a lot quieter.'

Alarm bells had started to ring, but I wanted to hear him out. 'And why would quiet be important?'

'It'll make sense when you hear what I have to tell you.'

I had to make a quick judgement call. For some reason, Alan was uncomfortable being here in the building with so many others. It wasn't the first time a client had said that to me, but given that someone was now saying those words in a hostile tone, was being alone with him a risk I was willing to take? I did sometimes see clients on a Saturday morning and knew the place would be quiet then.

Alan looked like he was really struggling, and I felt the hostile tone came out of that struggle. I made a decision. 'Okay, I think I can accommodate that. Maybe we can meet on a Saturday morning.'

'That might work.' Alan didn't look any happier after that offer, but that was as good as I could do. I'd have to run it by Dorothy first.

'I have an idea what we might start with today if you're in agreement. I think we'll do a little grounding exercise.' This was something I often did with clients who appeared agitated.

'Grounding? How?' He was looking all tense again.

'Just go with it and see if it works, and if it doesn't, fair enough, but let me try. Now, follow my voice. We'll start with where you're sitting. I want you to feel yourself sitting in the chair. Notice the way your legs feel, solid on the ground, the way the chair holds you comfortably and securely.'

He was looking at me sceptically, but I went through the senses – sight, smell, touch, sound – and I discerned a gradual softening in his features. We spent about five minutes on the exercise, but as soon as it had finished, Alan was back on full alert. I was used to behaviour like his from traumatised patients. They found it so hard to settle into themselves, to find a peaceful place. The stress hormones were constantly being reactivated.

'That's great doing an exercise like that, but where does it get me?' he asked immediately after.

'It's been proven that if we can relax our bodies enough, it will give us time to heal.'

'Maybe I have too much to heal from. I think you'll agree when you hear what I have to tell you. I'm carrying a lot of guilt around.' He laughed. 'That's funny, isn't it? Someone who was treated like shit feels guilty. You'd think I'd be guilt-free after what I've been through.'

'What you're saying shows a lot of insight. You have self-awareness, and that will help you with the healing process.'

He guffawed when I said that. 'Sure, yeah, self-aware-ness... all the shit I had to deal with. I'm very aware of that and how messed up I am. Healing, that's gonna take a while, like about as long a while as it took me to get this messed up, and that was a long while, believe me.'

Our session went on like that, me offering hope and him shooting it down. What he had said about the guilt resonated with me, but obviously I couldn't share that with him. What I had seen my own mother go through haunted me. I had stood like a bystander – the peacemaker – and watched it happen to her. I had been a child for most of it, and then my father died. The drinking killed him before I had time to let him know my real feelings, so I was left with the guilt of not doing more to protect her. And that guilt came out in all sorts of ways – rage being one of them. Like the day I had waited for Gary outside his apartment and felt an urge to hurt someone badly so they would never bother me again. I saw something like that rage in Alan, emotions darting each way like a pinball, bouncing from one thing to another and never settling, never having that resting place inside him.

I went for lunch and took a stroll in the park, sat on my usual bench, listened to the birds, enjoyed the peace and tranquility. And then my phone rang.

I could see from the caller ID that it was one of my fellow counsellors called Irene.

'Hello, yeah?' I said tentatively. Irene only called when it was something work related.

'I think you need to get back here quickly, Nicole. Dorothy is looking to speak with you.' She whispered this last bit as if she was afraid of being overheard.

'What? Why? It's lunchtime. Did a client show up early or something?'

'No, it's not that. It's something else. Files. Your files were found outside. Someone spotted them on your car.'

'*On* my car?' Had I heard that right? 'But I haven't been at my car since this morning.'

Suddenly an ominous feeling overcame me, a sense of dread that something nasty was unfolding.

'Okay, thanks, Irene, I'm coming back now.'

I walked quickly back to work, my body stiff with tension. Nearing the building, that tension increased so much that my mouth was dry, and my heart was hammering in my chest. I looked up the steps to the big front door, the one that I was shortly going to knock on, because Dorothy's office was just inside the door.

A sense of dread almost glued my feet to the ground. I didn't want to go up there. I'd had enough. First the missing clock, then the person shining the torch in my office window late at night, then the creepy incident at the zoo. I was sure whatever had happened with the files would be connected, and I just didn't want to face it. Enough was enough. Right there and then, I felt like turning around and just walking away, but then I thought that would be giving in to whoever was doing this.

Whatever their motive, I couldn't just fold and let them win.

So step by stone step I climbed up to the big wooden door

and pressed on the bell, which rang with a startled shrill. Dorothy answered with a stony countenance, turned and walked back into her office, not bothering to check if I was following. I walked sheepishly in after her, even though I knew I had done nothing wrong. Memories of my session with Alan flooded my mind, and our talk of guilt felt like a presence beside me.

'These are yours?' Dorothy was waving a couple of Manila folders in the air.

'I'm not sure,' I replied honestly. 'Lots of counsellors use Manila folders to keep individual counselling files in.' I was pretending to know nothing about this so Irene wouldn't get into trouble for telling me. I walked towards Dorothy to take them, but she kept the files in the air, like she didn't want to give them to me yet.

She turned one of the folders around so I could see the client name written on the front. 'Recognise the name?'

It was one of my clients. 'Yes, I do, but where did you find it? That was in my filing cabinet. I haven't seen that client for over a week.'

'I found it in the same place as this one.' She turned the second folder around so I could see the name – another one of my clients.

'I'll tell you where I found them, Nicole, or rather, where they were found – on the roof of your car. That's where. They could have easily blown open and the contents scattered all over the car park before we had a chance to collect them. And you know what that would mean if notes on our clients got out in the public domain?'

'That would be a disaster, of course, but I didn't leave them there. I don't know how that happened.'

'It would be a disaster, yes, possibly the end of this prac- tice, which I have painstakingly built up over many years, that's what it would be. Our clients would sue for breach of confidentiality, and rightly so.'

'But I don't know how they got there.' Anger surged up inside me now. Dorothy was presenting this apocalyptic scenario, and she was holding me directly responsible.

'Can you think of any other way they might have got there, then? The roof of your car. I've seen you go out to it to smoke now and again. You probably bring some files to scan through while you're there. No?'

It was true that on rare occasions I had taken files out with me just as far as the car, but that was only for patients I was seeing that day. Neither of the files Dorothy had shown me were patients I was about to see.

'It makes no sense to me,' I said eventually.

'It makes no sense to me either, but we have the evidence right in front of us.' Dorothy held the files up again for emphasis. She put them down on the table.

'Nicole, are you okay?' Dorothy asked me in a softer voice, but her eyes were still cold.

'Of course I'm okay, but there's been stuff happening, and I can't explain it. Like the keys going missing, and one evening, there was somebody outside the building shining a torch into my office, and then someone has been damaging my neighbour's property and making it look like it's me.'

I could see Dorothy almost physically backing off as I reeled out the list of incidents. She jerked her head back and gave me a quizzical look.

'Yeah, I know it sounds crazy, but all those things did happen. It feels like the time I was stalked, but I don't know who is doing this. I've no idea.'

Dorothy softened her expression. 'Nicole, do you think you had enough counselling after the stalking incident?'

'I believe I did, and I put a good self-care plan in place. I think I know when I am back on an even keel.'

'Do you? It's obviously so important in our profession.'

'Well, I see you for supervision, and there haven't been any alarm bells ringing, have there?'

'The jury's out on that one after today. It can take time, as we both know, for PTSD to manifest. It can be triggered without our even being aware of it.'

'I am fine to carry out my duties. The stuff going on is external and has nothing to do with the way I see the world. If you think I need to be assessed, then I'll go with that, but for the moment I am quite capable of carrying out my duties.'

'And the files?' Dorothy picked them up.

'I don't know what happened there, but I will look into it.'

I took the files from her. She didn't quite hand them to me, and I didn't quite take them politely. I was feeling angry. Something occurred to me in that moment. Whoever had taken my keys must have accessed my office without being seen and taken the files from the filing cabinet.

I went straight downstairs and found Magda, the cleaner, in the kitchen.

'Magda, did you see anyone strange in the building today at lunchtime?'

Magda frowned and shook her head. 'No, nobody strange. I cleaning all the morning and nothing, but I in and out, you know. Upstairs too. Don't see everything.'

Magda was looking at me in a strange way. I felt like she was also assessing my mental state. I had asked her about the clock and now was asking again about strangers in the building.

I began to doubt that I hadn't taken the files out there, but I knew I hadn't. Self-belief was my only hope. I was being targeted. I had to fight back.

16

DANIEL

I decided to tell Pamela about the new information on Pablo. She was my partner and the person who looked after Ben when I wasn't there. If there was any possibility that Pablo's past could pose a threat to Ben, she needed to know.

I broached the subject once Ben had gone to bed and we were relaxing on the couch.

'You know what you were saying about Pablo in the restaurant that night and why he came to Europe to work. Well, it turns out he has a very good reason.'

Pamela perked up when I said that. 'Oh yeah? What's that?'

'He had to go into hiding.'

'Sounds dodgy.'

'Not his fault though. It's his brother, got mixed up with a gang. They're not Spanish at all. They're from Guatemala.'

Pamela was shaking her head. 'That all sounds a bit hard to believe.'

'Well, we know there's something up because he was

secretly talking about plans, so he had something to hide. We have to work on the assumption it might be true.'

'That's got worrying implications for a few things, Ben being the first of them.'

'That's exactly what I was thinking.'

'Nicole's state of mind is the other,' said Pamela. 'If he sees her as an easy mark, then maybe he's using her, dragging her into the whole thing. If that's true, then what does he want from her?'

'I don't know, but, as you say, with Nicole's state of mind, she could be easy pickings. I want you to keep an eye out, be extra vigilant around Ben. We need to keep him as far away from all this as we can.'

'You need to protect yourself too, Daniel. If he is using Nicole, then the maintenance money you're paying... where's that going? He's in a desperate situation. Maybe he's got some excuse ready to get his hands on that.'

'I don't think Nicole would be that foolish to give him access.'

'Yeah, but she's mad about him, or at least the person he's pretending to be. You shouldn't be naïve. He could be up to anything.'

'It's Ben I'm concerned about, and that's where the focus needs to stay. I decided I need to be more proactive in protecting him. I'm going to do a little research myself and see if I can find out more information about Pablo. If he is up to something more than what he's telling Nicole, then we need to know. I'm going to follow him and see what he's doing when she's not around.'

Pamela frowned. 'Is that safe?'

'I'll be careful. It's Ben and Nicole's safety I'm worried about. There've been other things happening I didn't want to tell you about, but when Nicole took Ben to the zoo on Satur-day, she told me someone tried to lure Ben away. They'd dropped money in a bag at his feet and hurried off towards the entrance.'

Pamela rolled her eyes. 'That sounds as farfetched a story as you can get. It could have been a complete accident. I mean, people drop money all the time.'

'But the way they hurried off and then disappeared struck me as odd too.'

'Ah c'mon, Daniel... Nicole is taking this all a bit too far now. She definitely hasn't fully recovered from her stalking incident.'

The way Pamela said it with such conviction made me doubt Nicole's version. Maybe Nicole had imagined these events, somehow turned into a fantasist. That made me even more determined to check up on Pablo. If she was prone to exaggeration, she was leaving herself wide open to exploitation.

I put my plan into action the following evening after work. I took up a position just down the road from Pablo's school. It was an old building in a city centre location, so there were plenty of shop doorways to hide in.

Pressing in close to one of those doorways, I waited patiently for 8pm to roll around. That was when most evening classes finished. Sure enough, at 8.10pm, a small group of students spilled out of the school, lighting cigarettes, chatting and saying goodbye. Shortly afterwards, I saw Pablo emerge and stand on the high, concrete steps to light a cigarette before hurrying down the street in my direction.

That I hadn't accounted for.

As far as I knew, he had an apartment not too far from the school, but in the opposite direction to where I stood. He carried a dark bag over one shoulder. I squeezed in tight to the doorway and held my breath. He marched past on the other side of the street, looking straight ahead, seemingly focused on wherever he was going.

Once he was fifty metres ahead of me, I emerged from my hiding place and walked tentatively after him, keeping to my side of the street. He kept walking for another few minutes before stopping and ducking into a convenience store.

He came out a couple of minutes later and looked both ways before turning right and heading up a side street. I walked quickly to the corner of the side street and reached it just in time to see him ring a bell, wait. A buzzer sounded, and he pushed a door to a block of apartments open. He disappeared inside.

I took note of the name of the street and the name of the apartment block before going back to the corner of the street and waiting, just out of sight. I checked every now and then to see if he came back out, but he didn't.

I left for home twenty minutes later.

'YOU'RE LATE,' Pamela observed when I walked in.

'Sorry, I was checking on our friend Pablo. Turns out he went to some random apartment block after work.'

'That doesn't tell you much. Could just be a friend.'

'I don't know. Something about the way he was acting – looking around him – made me think it was a bit more than that. You could be right of course, but he ducked into a convenience store on the way, and he checked to see who was around before turning up the street to the apartment block.'

'Maybe he's two-timing Nicole.'

'Maybe, but I'm going to see if I can find out who lives there. There might be a couple of late nights for a while, Pamela. I really want to get to the bottom of this.'

'Then you really need to be careful. If he is mixed up with some dodgy people, you don't want to get too close.'

'That's why I'm doing this. If he is mixed up with dodgy people, I don't want him around Nicole or my son.'

17

NICOLE

Finally, the locks both at work and at my house had been changed. I felt a small degree of safety once more. But I still felt uneasy that someone had gained access to my office, and what's more, they wanted me to know that they had gained access. First, the clock disappearing and then the files, which had been found. Subtle ways of showing me someone had my keys, and that they were enjoying toying with my sense of security. All I could do was wonder what they were going to do next.

I didn't have to wait too long to find out.

The day passed in a bit of a blur. Ben was coming over later, and I hadn't had time to prepare any food, so I went to the local shops at lunchtime and got a tray of lasagne that I could just pop in the oven as soon as I got home. I got some butterhead lettuce and cucumber too, wanting to add some vegetables to the meal, even though I knew Ben would turn his nose up at it. He was a typical kid in that respect. He liked food with plenty of carbs and meat. To him, lettuce was rabbit food.

I still added vegetables whenever I could, hoping that one

day he would see the light. I suspected that day was still some time off.

I had supervision with Dorothy later in the afternoon and was dreading it. We hadn't spoken since the files had been found on my car. As soon as I sat down in her office, I made sure to start with the good news.

'The locks downstairs have been changed. Here's a spare set of keys.' I slid the keys across her desk.

She took them and looked over her glasses at me. 'I hope that's an end to these mishaps. They seem to be happening with increasing frequency.'

'I'm sure it is.'

I didn't know how much conviction there was in my voice. I certainly didn't feel it was the end, but I didn't want to tell Dorothy about the other things that had been going on. She had questioned my mental state, and I wanted to present as a reasonable and capable individual.

Dorothy raised her eyebrows, so they formed two perfect arches, and tilted her head to the side. 'How are you getting on with your clients?'

She waited for my answer. Dorothy had a counsellor's knack for keeping silent after an open question, creating a void I felt the need to fill.

'Things are going well, generally. I'm still in a bit of a deadlock with that young man Alan. He has something to disclose, but he's taking his time about it. There's a lot of anger and hurt there, so I'm not surprised. He says he'll disclose soon, but he wants to see me at a time that's quieter.'

'Oh.' Dorothy's eyebrows rose a little more, and her eyes widened.

'Yes, I told him I could see him on Saturday morning. I have seen clients before on that day when I felt it was necessary. With him I think it is. I don't think we can make a break-through until he fully discloses his past.'

Dorothy shook her head. 'Given your state of mind at the moment, do you really think you should see clients out of hours?'

'I think my mind is absolutely fine, and I trust my judgement. There are usually one or two others working here on Saturdays. I won't be completely alone.'

'I can't be here, as I have weekend commitments. I'm not happy just to let you go ahead with your session without me.'

'I'll be fine, honest. I'll make sure someone else is around. I have nothing formal in the diary yet anyway, so no point in discussing it further until that happens.'

'Agreed. But keep me informed. This is my practice, and I need to know what's going on.'

I packed up for home after my check-in with Dorothy, thinking that if Alan really wanted to see me on a Saturday, then I might just go ahead whatever Dorothy said. She didn't seem keen, and I was intrigued by his case. I wanted to make that breakthrough. Maybe it was how his case reminded me of my own past. I could relate to him and didn't want to see him suffer any longer than he needed to.

It was a little later than usual by the time I hit the road. Daylight was slowly turning to dusk. I turned on the news channel in my car, but soon tired of the serious topics and switched to some lighter chart music on another station. The occasional chatter of the DJs was irritating, but, on balance, it was the better pick.

The drive home took about thirty minutes if I avoided traffic jams, so I took my usual route through a couple of housing estates and up narrow streets with light traffic.

It was while driving on one of these quieter streets that I noticed a car behind me. It seemed to be sticking close by. Since I was taking a route through the back roads, it surprised me that every time I took a new turn, so did the car.

I assured myself it was just a coincidence. At the same

time I sped up a little, but the car stayed close to me. In the fading light, it was hard to make out who was driving, but I could see it was just one person in the car. They looked to be wearing dark clothing and a dark baseball cap. That jolted a memory of the person at the zoo. Ben had said they'd been dressed in dark clothes.

I took a deep breath to calm myself. After all that had happened, it was hard not to jump to the wrong conclusion. I decided to test my gut feeling by taking a turn down an offbeat road. The car followed.

Now I was scared.

My hands gripped the steering wheel, and my feet felt clumsy as they worked the clutch and accelerator.

Okay, stay calm, don't do anything rash, and most of all don't crash, I told myself. The most important thing was to get home. If this was somebody trying to spook me, surely they would take off once I reached my house. There would be neighbours around. I could easily call for help.

But what if there weren't neighbours around? Even if James next door was there, what would he make of me pulling up and shouting for help? He might pretend not to hear. At best, he thought I was a loose cannon, at worst a stalker.

No, I needed to think clearly. Where was the best place to go? Then it occurred to me. On my route home, I sometimes passed a police station. If I could find my way there safely, then surely the person following would see my intention and drive off.

I fumbled with my phone, which was in my bag on the passenger seat, checking the rearview mirror as I did. The fading light made it hard to see what I was doing. Then the person behind switched their lights to full beam, making it impossible to see the driver. I swiped the screen to activate the phone, and pulled up Google maps before nervously keying in the words 'Garda station', all the while trying not to crash. The robotic maps voice kicked in, telling me exactly where to go.

That calmed me slightly. I wouldn't take a wrong turn now and end up in a cul-de-sac with no way out.

I approached a big intersection with traffic lights. The voice was telling me to drive straight on. The lights were orange, about to turn red. I gunned it, but as I got close to the lights, they switched colour, and I had to stop. Cars were already moving across the intersection. There was no chance for me to sneak across. I would have to wait, with the chasing car somewhere behind me.

I drummed my fingers impatiently on the steering wheel.

'Come on, come on,' I pleaded with the traffic lights.

I checked in my rearview mirror, and sure enough, the car was right behind me, as close as it could be. The driver dressed in dark clothes and a baseball cap. As far as I could make out, they also had sunglasses on. At dusk?

The appearance was chilling. I felt vulnerable sitting in my car, afraid to jump out and run, afraid to stay where I was. Then I felt a gentle bump against the back of my car, enough to jolt the car, and then another bump, this one a little firmer.

I felt my car move. Even with the brakes applied, the car behind – clearly heavier than mine – was nudging me into traffic. My lighter car inched towards the red light, towards the stream of traffic that was racing across the intersection in front of me.

Panicked, I slammed my foot on the brake and pulled up the handbrake. My car stopped, but I heard a grinding noise behind me as the other car continued to nudge me on.

'Stop,' I shouted. 'Stop... what the hell are you doing?'

Despite both brake and handbrake being engaged, the car pushed me farther and farther out until the stream of traffic was only metres away. One of the cars that flew past beeped at me, as if they thought I was just rolling out into the traffic. I could hear the driver behind me revving, and with the sound, my car was pushed even farther out.

I started to cry, tears rolling down my cheeks, as the helplessness of my situation hit me. If I didn't do something soon, I was going to hit another car. As if to prove that point, a truck flew past, its huge wheels passing just feet from my bumper.

Then the tears dried up, and the anger flowed through me – the same raw anger I had felt with Gary. It was cold and calculated and would eliminate the threat, no matter what the consequences for me.

I looked behind me. There was a big wheel wrench in the boot for taking the wheels off. It was heavy enough to do serious damage and light enough for me to use. My car was a hatchback, so I made a plan to access the boot by crawling through the back seat. When I got the wrench, I would use it to smash the windscreen of the car pursuing me, to stop the person from easily getting away; then I was going to smash their side window so I could get at them.

The rage gave me a kind of calm, even though the car was still shoving me slowly out into the oncoming traffic. I looked in the rearview mirror and saw the darkly dressed figure behind me, like a hunter zoning in on their prey.

Calmly, I took my seat belt off. I was just about to lever myself from my seat and into the back of the car when I noticed the cars at the other intersections had stopped. Their lights were red. Mine was green. A different instinct kicked in, and I pressed my foot hard on the accelerator. My car jerked forward, but quickly picked up speed until I was tearing away.

I got a better look at the car that had been pushing me. It was white in colour and had some sort of writing on the side. Even as I looked at it, I saw it turn and take off up a different road to mine. I immediately pulled in to the side of the road, switched my engine off and dropped my head onto the cool leather of the steering wheel.

The tears came again, in a gushing waterfall this time, and I snatched at breaths as I tried to inhale. Fear of having a complete panic attack gripped me. My body was tensed up, and my heart was pounding in my chest. It would subside. I knew that, but how long would it take, and would whoever had been following me come back?

When my body finally relaxed enough and the tears had turned to a trickle, I started the car and drove, keeping the maps on my phone active, certain of where I wanted to go. The police station was only half a kilometre away, and I felt a surge of relief when I saw its grey, characterless features and the familiar blue sign outside.

I climbed from the car, my legs so stiff with tension it was hard to walk. I staggered to the front door and pushed it open. Inside was a bare reception counter, and behind that, a Garda was filling out a form. He was in his late twenties with dark hair that was already receding, and a pleasant, open face.

'Someone followed my car and tried to push me out into traffic,' I blurted.

The Garda's expression hardly changed, but he put the pen he was using down on the counter.

'Do you wish to report an incident?' he asked in a gentle voice.

'Yes, I certainly do. Somebody was trying to kill me.'

He reached behind and grabbed a form from a pile there. 'Okay, let's get some details. Your name and address, and tell me exactly what happened.'

He wrote while I recounted the incident. When I finished, I told him about my previous stalker and how the police had been called on Gary Mulligan.

'Do you have reason to believe the same individual may be involved this time?' he asked.

'I really don't know, but he was in Dublin recently. He called in to my ex.'

'Your ex?' The Garda raised a brow.

'Yes, he had stalked him too before.'

The Garda slid the form over to me and got me to sign it.

'Okay, let's take a look at the car,' he said, and came out from behind the counter. Outside, he checked the front of the car first before going around to the back. He bent over and ran a hand over the rear bumper. 'Hmm, couple of bumps and scratches there alright. Have you had any recent accidents?'

'No,' I replied a little too sharply.

The Garda smiled. 'I'm not doubting your story, just double-checking these bumps weren't caused by something else.'

'No. Some lunatic tried to shove me into the path of oncoming traffic.'

The Garda nodded. 'Okay, I have all the details now, and we'll look into it. We'll be in touch if we find anything significant. There should be CCTV footage on the intersection, so we'll at least see the make of the car.'

I was about to get into my car when he stopped and looked at me. 'Are you okay to drive home?'

The question made me take a deep breath. I could feel tears welling up again, but I nodded and climbed into the car. Somewhere in the back of my mind, I was thinking of the lasagne I had bought for Ben and how I needed to get home in time to put it on.

The drive back was nerve-racking, as I checked my mirrors constantly, but I made it home. I felt a massive surge of relief when I finally pulled into my drive.

18

DANIEL

Nicole was in a state of shock when I dropped Ben over. She tried to hide it as best she could for his sake, but I could see her strained look. Once Ben had gone into the sitting room to do his homework, we stayed in the kitchen and talked.

'A car followed me from work. They tried to push me out into traffic. I could have been killed,' she said quietly. Her voice was measured, but I could hear a crack, like she was going to burst into tears any moment.

'I went to the Gardai,' she continued. 'They had a look at the car and could see some bumps and scratches where the other car had pushed me.'

I couldn't believe it. 'Did you see who it was?'

'No, they were wearing dark clothes and a baseball cap, and it was impossible to see details.'

'Dark clothes, like the person at the zoo.'

Nicole nodded. 'Exactly. It must have been the same person.'

'So who could it be?'

It seemed like someone was deliberately taunting or

trying to menace Nicole, but why? In the back of my mind was the question as to how much her previous trauma was affecting her perspective as well.

'Do you have any idea who it might be? Why someone would be stalking you like this? Could it be Gary out for revenge? He certainly has good reason to keep his identity hidden.'

I wondered as well if it had any connection with Pablo, but I didn't want to say that. That was a line of enquiry I was going to have to pursue myself. If or when I got any evidence, I would present it to her.

With that decision made, I left Nicole. She was expecting Pablo over later, she told me, but not till about 10pm. She said he was going to the gym after class, and I decided it was my opportunity to check that was where he really was.

At 8pm, I positioned myself in the same spot as before, buried in the shadows of that same shopfront. Just like last time, there was a huddle of students on the big stone steps. Pablo walked briskly past them, pausing momentarily to light a cigarette before walking in the direction where I was hiding. Pushing myself farther into the doorway, I watched him walk straight past on the other side. This time, he didn't drop in to the convenience store. He kept going, reaching the bottom of the small street he had turned at before. Again, he checked up and down the main street before entering it.

That's not normal, I thought. *People don't make a regular habit of checking up and down before walking up a street. Something is definitely up here.*

When Pablo disappeared up the small street, I hurried over to the corner and took a swift look down to see him standing outside the same block of apartments. When the buzzer sounded, he went inside. I waited a few minutes, then walked slowly up the street. It was narrow with a path on one side and cars parked on the other. There was barely the width of a car between the parked cars and the path.

Walking carefully, and prepared to hide if I had to, I reached the entrance of the apartments. Through a glass door I could see a hallway, and to the right of that a series of postboxes. The hall was cramped but reasonably well kept. Looking to my right, I saw the various buzzers for the doors, some with names underneath, some with just apartment numbers. Scanning through them, I saw a variety of surnames, many of them foreign. But that was standard for the city centre. Like most cities, it was where the younger migrant communities lived, close to work and to all amenities.

I was standing there, thinking it all through, when I heard a distinct metallic sound come from inside. It took me a few seconds to realise it was the sound of lift doors opening. Someone came out of the lift. I had a second to dash from the doorway.

So I ran, not seeing who it was. I didn't want to take any chances. The distance to the end of the street would take too long for me to cover before whoever it was came out. There was no other choice, so I ducked behind one of the parked cars and waited. The door opened with a metallic squeak, and I heard what sounded like Spanish being spoken.

So it is Pablo, I thought.

The voices were coming closer to me. As they neared, I shimmied around to the side of the car that was facing away from the buildings, making sure to stay as low as I could. Footsteps and the voices passed within a few feet of me; then they grew more distant.

Staying low, I inched out from behind the car to get a view down the street. I could see Pablo's back. With him were two other guys. They looked to be of a similar age and height, but from my position, that was all I could make out.

Nothing too unusual there, I thought, *Pablo out visiting a couple of friends.* The problem was that he had told Nicole he was going to the gym. I decided to double-check that wasn't still the case, that he was on his way there, but it was already getting late. He was due at Nicole's at 10pm.

Following at a discreet distance, I saw them walk about two hundred metres down the main street before ducking into an internet café.

That's strange, I thought, *all of them together.* I gave it a few minutes, and when I saw no sign of them coming out, I walked quickly past the window of the café and glanced inside. The three of them were gathered around just the one PC, and one of them had earbuds in. I kept on walking, returning to where I had my car parked, and sat inside it, thinking through the events of the night.

So Pablo definitely wasn't going to the gym but instead had met up with a couple of Spanish-speaking friends. No big deal if he had changed his plans, but if he hadn't and was deliberately lying to Nicole about what he was doing, then it was a big deal.

Arriving home, I felt the urge to tell Pamela, even though I didn't want to stoke any more animosity between her and Nicole. Still, I had to bounce what I'd seen off someone.

Pamela nodded after I told her. 'He told Nicole he was going to the gym and then ended up huddled around a screen in an internet café. Sounds dodgy. Why go to an internet café? Everyone has access to the internet... unless you wanted to hide your IP address?'

Exactly the same thoughts had been going through my mind. 'We shouldn't jump to conclusions though. If he is in hiding, then that's an obvious way to disguise your location. Could be something innocent though, a chance for him and his friends to get on a group chat.'

'Maybe, but he could be up to something dodgy too,'

Pamela said. 'Is he running away from trouble back at home, or is he knee-deep in trouble over here? Could be a double bluff to get our sympathy, using the cover of a seemingly normal life and relationship to hide whatever he's up to.'

I knew Pamela would jump to the worst-case scenario, but I also had serious doubts about Nicole's judgement on Pablo, especially if she was still suffering from the trauma of her prior incident.

'You need to seriously think about Ben,' Pamela continued. 'Do you really think Nicole's place is suitable at the moment? Pablo spends a lot of time there. Until we know what he's up to, it doesn't seem like a safe place to me.'

19

NICOLE

I was left badly shaken by the incident with the car but determined to live my life as close to normal as possible. Ben had loved the lasagne and that had cheered me up after a horrible day. Pablo came over at 10pm, and I felt secure having him around.

I told him about the incident.

'You had a hard time today, I can see it,' he said as we sat on the couch. He ran his fingers through my hair and down my face. They felt warm and comforting. 'That's pretty messed up what happened to you today. I really hope the Gardaí get that person. You deserve a nice life. You're a good person. This kind of thing shouldn't be happening to you.'

I snuggled into him, grateful for the comforting words. I felt exactly the same way. What had I done to deserve this after all I had been through?

'Thank you,' I said. 'Pablo, maybe you should think about staying here more. I feel safe when you're around.'

Pablo smiled. 'Hey, you read my mind. I was gonna say something to you, but you didn't seem in a good way, so I said nothing. But now you tell me this, maybe it's time to say what I want.'

Pablo took a deep breath and glanced at me, almost sheepishly, his brown eyes melting me.

'Nicole, I get to know you well over the past six months, and I like so many things about you... no, I love so many things about you. You make me happy and like I feel I am really at home and at peace, first time in a long time.' He jumped up off the couch and ran over to his bag, pulled out a small box and raced back to the couch. He opened it, and I saw a beautiful emerald ring inside.

'I wanted to get you this ring,' he said. 'It's not pressure or something too serious, but Nicole, I am serious about you, and I wanted you to know that.'

'That's so beautiful, Pablo. You are so kind and exactly what I need in my life right now.'

'No, you are exactly what I need in my life right now.' He leaned over and kissed me for the longest time. During that lingering moment, the world was set right again.

I tried to put the thoughts of what had happened today out of my mind. It was something the Gardaí were going to be following up on. I had faith they would find something. The Garda at the station had said there were CCTV cameras around major junctions. It was just a question of them reviewing the tapes and finding the car.

The next morning at work passed for as close to normal as it could. I had bought a small digital clock to replace my grandparents' wooden one. The digital version didn't give off the same homey effect, but it would have to do for the moment.

At lunchtime, I strolled to the nearby shop to get a wrap and juice, eager to get to my sanctuary in the park for some proper chill-out time. I was just leaving the shop when I saw someone who made me stop in my tracks.

Alan, looking handsome and suave, was walking towards the shop door. I stayed put, realising there was no escaping him.

'Hey, Nicole, how are you?' he asked as he got closer.

'Grand, thanks.' I was a little unsure how to respond. He was a client, after all, and I didn't want to be too familiar with him. 'And you?'

The timing of the encounter had thrown me. It was on my lunch break, but it was a public space, and he was fully entitled to be there.

'Good, yeah.' He smiled with what looked like genuine warmth, but then he appeared stuck for follow-up conversation.

'Just out on lunch,' I said, trying to fill the gap for him.

'Right. Me too. I don't normally come around here, but I don't live too far away, and I'm on a day off.'

'Me too, as in I don't work too far away.' I pointed towards work, and we both laughed at that.

Then I saw Alan take a step back. He was looking at my pointing hand.

'Oooh, that's nice,' he said, nodding at the ring.

'Thanks, yes. My partner gave it to me, just yesterday actually. That's not the sort of thing guys notice straight away.'

Alan shook his head and smiled. 'The instincts of the charmer, that's what I have whether I like it or not.'

An awkward pause in the conversation followed, so I took the opportunity to make my excuses and go.

'I'd better get back to work. Enjoy your day off,' I said as I left.

'Yeah, no worries,' Alan said, but he stayed where he was, and when I turned, he was still watching me walk off.

It gave me an unsettling feeling, and I had second thoughts about going to the park alone. I didn't want that thought to take hold though, so I took my lunch to my usual spot on the bench, in among the trees, so I could listen to the blackbirds singing.

During the busy afternoon, I slipped out to my car and had what I promised myself would be my only smoke of the day. The meeting with Alan was playing on my mind, and I'd had to resist the urge to think about it during the counselling sessions.

I had to presume it was pure coincidence that we had bumped into each other at the shop. I'd checked his address afterwards, and he did indeed live within a mile of the area. There would be plenty of other shops that might be closer to him, but when people are out and about, they might just go to the nearest one at the time.

But then there was his overreaction to the ring. He had spotted it immediately. That wouldn't be that unusual, but his zeroing in on it had made me feel uncomfortable.

With Gary, I had noticed that his comments and observations had gradually become more personal, stepping over lines at times, testing boundaries. Then he had started the full-blown stalking. I had tried to keep the boundaries professional. It could be difficult, because of the personal details that clients revealed, but I felt I had managed his expectations quite well.

Finishing my smoke, I headed back inside and saw the last two clients of the afternoon. I was feeling pretty drained by then.

I was just tidying up the last of my files when there was a loud hammering on my door. I rushed to open it. Magda the cleaner was standing there, and she was pointing towards the car park, her face a mask of anxiety.

'There is problem with your car,' she blurted. I looked towards the car park. My car wasn't visible, but I caught an acrid smell, and I knew before I reached the back door what I would see.

As I ran out onto the gravel car park, I saw smoke billowing from my hatchback. It was a dirty, black, noxious cloud of brutal smoke that funneled out through the windows, which were already turning black and melting with the heat. I heard one of them pop, and shards of glass sprayed out to cover the ground.

'Stay back,' I said to Magda and pushed her inside.

I heard a door open upstairs and Dorothy shout, 'Oh my God, someone call the fire brigade.'

I already had my phone in hand and was dialing the number.

Sirens sounded a few minutes later. From the safety of the building, I could see flames licking through the clouds of smoke, their angry, orange-yellow tongues twisting towards the sky. All I could do was pray that the petrol tank wouldn't explode.

The fire brigade managed to get one of their trucks through the back entrance and into the car park. They quickly identified a water hydrant location and sprayed gallons of water all over the car until the roaring fire was reduced to a loud, steamy exhalation. The flames died down, and the acrid, black smoke turned to a greyish steam.

I ventured out once I saw the smoke and flames were dying down. My car was a blackened wreck, just the steel shell surviving. The inside was either burnt or twisted into unrecognisable shapes.

'Is that yours?' one of the firemen asked, nodding towards the car.

'Yes, it was me who made the call. I've no idea what happened.' That was true, but my mind couldn't help going back to the smoke I'd had earlier. I was pretty sure I'd squashed the butt of the cigarette under my shoe when I got out, but the area around the car was all blackened and burnt, so checking would be impossible.

Dorothy marched down the steps then. She had been observing the proceedings from the top of the steps. I felt myself stiffen as she approached.

'What do you think happened?' she addressed the fireman.

He looked over at the still-steaming burnt-out frame of the car. 'It's a write-off is what happened, but how it started I don't know. The Gardaí may come out and have a look. The insurance company almost certainly will. They'll want to know how it started before they pay out.'

'Have you any idea?' Dorothy turned to me. There wasn't a trace of empathy or warmth in her eyes.

'No, I don't, but I am very upset that my car has just gone up in smoke.'

'Of course you are. It's a terrible thing to happen,' Dorothy said. Her words sounded sympathetic, but I could see no sympathy in her expression. 'If there's anything we can help you with, let us know.'

The fireman looked from her to me. 'These things do happen. It's not the first, and it certainly won't be the last car fire we put out. Sometimes the electrics just go funny in them, and then you get a couple of sparks. Doesn't take much once the upholstery takes fire.'

'The question, I suppose, is how it caught fire in the first place,' Dorothy concluded and walked back up the stone steps.

I had to get in touch with the insurers, who said they'd have to examine the car. They would, however, give me a replacement car, as that was covered on my policy.

I had to get a taxi from work down to the car hire place, where they furnished me with a decent replacement. That much was resolved, but I was left with the question of how the fire had started. My mind kept going back to the missing keys – my car keys had been on that bunch. I'd had a spare key, so I hadn't changed the locks on the car. Now I was regretting that decision. I also thought back to the meeting with Alan that day.

I had a troubling sense that there might be a connection between the two events.

20

DANIEL

I didn't know what to say when Nicole phoned and told me about the car catching fire. First, I thought about her safety and that of Ben. If the fire had started slowly, it could have happened at any time. The results could have been far more serious. She told me she had been smoking in the car earlier, and that was the only thing she could think of. Again, I wondered about her state of mind. Was she finding it hard to concentrate and maybe forgetting to do simple things like put her cigarette out? I could hear how upset she was, so I said nothing.

I made a decision about one thing though, and I put it to her in as diplomatic a way as I could. With Ben tucked up in bed, I texted her and asked if she was able to take a call. She was.

'Are you feeling okay now?' I asked.

'Yep, Pablo is here. He's working on his laptop upstairs.'

'Great, it's been tough for you, Nicole, but this will all sort itself out. I'm sure the Gardaí will come up with evidence from that incident on the road, and it will let you know who is behind all this.'

'I hope they hurry up. I don't know how much more I can take.'

'I understand. Hopefully they will.' I paused then, because what I had to say next wasn't going to be easy. 'Nicole, with all of what's going on, I've been thinking about Ben. Do you think it would be an idea for him to stay over with me and Pamela a bit more, just for the moment, till all this is sorted?'

There was silence on the line before Nicole answered, 'What difference would that make?'

'It's just that he may be safer here is what I'm saying.'

'He's my son. I can look after him.'

'It's not you I'm thinking of. Of course you can look after him. It's just... what's been happening. It's a worry.'

'I know, Daniel. I'm worried too, but I don't think keeping a person I love away from me is going to help, do you?'

Nicole's voice was louder now. I didn't blame her for being angry, but I had to make my point.

'As I said, Nicole, it's just what's going on. A few different things have happened, and it seems to be getting worse.'

'All the more reason why I need family around me. If Ben suddenly starts to see less of me, he's going to wonder what's going on. You can't just brush it off with an explanation of someone wanting to harm his mother. That's going to worry him.'

'Okay, yeah, I see your point.'

We ended the conversation there. I didn't want to get into a full-blown argument about it. Nicole was going through a hard time. I didn't want to make it harder, but it didn't assuage my concerns over Ben.

'Penny for your thoughts?' Pamela had wandered in from the kitchen to join me on the couch.

'I was just talking to Nicole about what's been going on. I suggested to her about Ben staying over here more until it all blows over.' I had already told Pamela about the fire in the car.

'And?'

'Nicole wasn't into it. She reckons she needs family around now more than ever, and she thinks it might spook Ben as well.'

'But the question is, is she capable of looking after him at the moment? Like I said, you should be more insistent. Where is the maintenance money going? Is Nicole in a sound frame of mind to look after a ten-year-old?'

I heard footsteps in the hall outside, so I gestured for Pamela to stop talking.

'Ben?' I called. 'Is that you?'

He pushed the door to the living room open and poked a tousled head of hair in.

'I can't sleep.'

Pamela looked at me and raised her eyebrows. It was her way of telling me 'I told you so'.

I gestured Ben over, and he sat between me and Pamela on the couch. He was wearing light-blue pyjamas with cartoon space rockets all over them. It made me realise how much of a kid he still was.

'What's been keeping you awake, then?'

Ben yawned and stretched. 'I keep thinking about the person at the zoo.'

I could feel Pamela staring at me, but I didn't make eye contact with her.

'Oh, and what were you thinking?'

'I was thinking I hope they got their money back.'

'That's nice of you to be concerned about that.'

'Was there any other reason you were thinking about them?' Pamela asked.

'No, just it was weird.'

'Yes, it was weird,' Pamela agreed. 'Did it worry you at all?'

Behind Ben, I shook my head at Pamela.

Ben stretched again. 'No, not worry. Just thinking about the money, that's all.'

'Would you feel safer staying here more?' Pamela asked. Again I shook my head. Her questions were too much for a kid that age. It was something that needed to be worked out between the adults first.

Ben frowned. 'Here? Why?'

'I'm just wondering why you're not sleeping,' she said. 'Maybe it's something that's on your mind, and you might feel more comfortable here for a while.'

'No.' Ben shook his head adamantly. 'I want to be with my real mum.'

Pamela pulled back when he said that and didn't pursue the matter further.

'You have nothing to worry about,' I said to him and rubbed his head gently.

He leaned heavily into me then, and pretty soon his eyes closed, and his breathing became slower and deeper. I picked him up and carried him back to his bed.

When I returned to Pamela, she was glaring at me. 'You undermined me there,' she said. I could see real fire in her eyes.

'I didn't mean to. I just didn't want him more worried than he is.'

'You heard what he said about wanting to be with his *real* mum. Maybe I'm just getting in the way around here.'

I sat beside her and tried to put an arm around her, but she pulled away.

'You know that's not the case, but it's always going to be a bit of a balancing act where he's concerned.'

'Always sounds like a very long time. I'm not sure my patience can stretch that far.'

'You've been very good so far, Pamela. I know it's not easy to adapt.'

Thinking about it later, I felt caught between two things – my new life with Pamela and my old life with Nicole. Ben was in the middle, and my priority was to ensure he wasn't damaged or spooked by what was going on. Pamela's position I could completely understand too. She had been put in the middle of something that was not of her doing. But I was afraid that Ben might start kicking up against her if Pamela suggested again he spend less time with Nicole.

His safety was my main concern, and I wasn't willing to gamble with it. So many things had been happening in and around Nicole. It was just a question of time before Ben got caught up in it.

I resolved that I was going to do my best to shield him from that. If that meant getting more involved and figuring out what was going on with Nicole, then so be it. I had already started by checking up on Pablo.

There was something dodgy going on there – of that I had no doubt. The question was if it was connected to the nasty stuff that had been happening to Nicole.

If I had to be more proactive checking Pablo's story, then so be it.

21

NICOLE

The next day at work was stressful. Dorothy was giving me the cold shoulder, obviously thinking that I was to blame for my car going on fire. That annoyed and disappointed me. She was a counsellor first, a boss second. Surely a bit more empathy wouldn't have gone astray? Okay, she had her responsibilities as the boss, and my keys had gone missing, the files had been found and then the fire, but surely that pointed to an outside agency working against me, not that I was to blame.

I put my anger aside to make sure my perspective was as balanced as it could be for my clients. As counsellors, we had to be wary of not dragging our own baggage into the sessions. That was where Dorothy was supposed to help as supervisor, but she obviously wasn't in a frame of mind to do that.

I headed home after work, had a small bite to eat and went to the swimming pool for the last swim of the evening. It was dark by the time I got there, and the place was virtually empty save a single lifeguard, who was doubling up as receptionist. That suited me fine. There was nothing I liked better than having the pool to myself and not having to worry about bumping into people or, while swimming in a lane, having to speed up so I didn't get in anyone's way.

I usually did a dozen laps of front crawl, followed by a dozen of breaststroke, all at a leisurely pace. That was the part I enjoyed most, my head above the water, watching the lights dancing on the water as it rippled with my movement.

It was while I was doing this, lost in the rhythm of movement, that I heard noise somewhere behind me. The lights suddenly went off. The pool was instantly thrown into complete darkness, turning the water black. The whole place became a dark void, no longer giving me the security of being able to see the three-dimensional world. I stopped and treaded water, turning hopelessly in the direction of the noise I had heard.

'Hello?' I shouted. 'Is there anybody there?'

The silence that greeted me was worse than any noise I might have heard. It was an empty, menacing silence.

'Hello,' I shouted again. Still that deathly silence.

I was tempted to paddle over to the edge of the pool, just so I could feel something tangible, but my instincts told me to stay where I was. At least in the water I would hear somebody getting in. I was a strong swimmer, so a person would have to be equally strong to catch me.

I waited and listened. Each passing second was laden with a million possible dangers, and I couldn't tread water forever. If there was somebody waiting for me, they would know that. I'd be exhausted by the time I got out, helpless. They would have me exactly where they wanted me.

Then, as suddenly as the lights went out, they blasted back on again, blinding me in the pool so much that I had to shield my eyes. The glare of the light rushed my senses so I felt like I would start to go under. Then mercifully, I heard a call from the side of the pool.

'Hey, are you okay in there?' It was the lifeguard, and he

was hurrying along the edge of the pool towards me. The sight of his yellow top and red shorts sent a wave of relief through me. I swam the couple of strokes to the side and hauled myself out. I was shaking as I sat on the edge of the pool, my feet dangling in the water.

'Are you okay?' he repeated. He was a young guy, early twenties. He looked pale, standing back from me, as if unsure of what to do.

'I'm fine,' I managed to say while the shaking continued. 'I just got a fright when the lights went out.'

He was shaking his head and looking over at the entrance. 'I don't know what happened. My car alarm went off, and I ran out to check it. Next thing, when I came in, the lights were off. I didn't see anyone, but you sometimes get young guys messing around this time of night.'

He looked scared, like he knew he shouldn't have left the building.

'It's okay,' I said. 'These things happen. Probably just somebody messing about, all right. You had to go and check your car. Don't worry.'

He looked relieved when I said that. 'Thanks.'

Walking to the ladies' changing room was nerve-racking. I stood at the door and listened. Whoever had been in could have slipped in there. I heard no sound.

I entered and changed at the speed of light, then passed the still relieved-looking lifeguard to hurry to my car. I looked around but saw nothing. So I gunned the engine and tore out of the car park. It was only when I was a good bit up the road that I started to breathe easy again.

It could, as the lifeguard had said, been some young fellas messing about, but the whole thing had a more sinister feel to it. If it had been young lads, then there would have been a bit of sniggering. I had heard only eerie silence after the lights went out. Whoever it was wanted to scare me, and they certainly succeeded.

I had to put a brave face on when Daniel dropped Ben over. I said nothing about the event to Daniel. He had heard enough spooky stories from me. This was something I had to sort out myself. I needed to get to the bottom of what was going on. Whoever was doing it could have left a clue. They couldn't stay hidden all the time. Maybe the Gardaí would come up with something. I just had to try to hold my nerve for a little longer.

Ben was standoffish with me. The hug he gave me in return was limp. I thought maybe I had transferred my own shaky state onto him, so I was extra attentive and put a positive face on. Pablo wasn't coming over, so it was just me and Ben tonight.

'Let's watch some junk on TV while we have dinner,' I suggested.

'What sort of junk?' he asked moodily.

'Whatever type you like.'

'It's mostly adult stuff on this time of night, like news and that.'

'Okay, but we can check Netflix out. What programmes do you like at the moment?'

He shook his head. 'You wouldn't like any of my programmes.'

I was beginning to wilt under his negativity. My enthusiasm was quickly being replaced with exhaustion. My fear from earlier had worn off, and I guessed the adrenaline had dried up too. 'Okay, let's just flick it on and watch whatever comes up.'

Whatever came up was a quiz, and it engaged him for a few minutes only. The questions were too hard for him, so he started stretching and looking around once we had eaten our dinner.

I tried not to let the scene in the swimming pool replay in my mind, determined to put the incident down to a few young boys up to mischief.

'Mam,' Ben said lazily.

'Yes, love?' I replied.

'Some of the guys in my class have phones.'

'Oh.' I expected this would come up eventually, so I was half-prepared.

'They got them for their birthdays. We're all turning eleven this year.'

'So you are. Getting into the pre-teens. I'd better watch out,' I said cheerily.

'No, Mam, I'm serious. Some of the guys are getting phones. Can I get one too? I'll be eleven soon.'

'For me eleven is too young. You'll have plenty of time to get a phone. Enjoy your childhood while you can.'

'But phones *are* a part of childhood now,' he said grumpily.

'Not in my book,' I replied too sharply. I needed to wean him off the idea gently, but I was too tired.

He folded his arms deliberately and set his face into what he interpreted to be a look of anger. 'Pamela says I shouldn't spend so much time here,' he blurted out. 'She thinks it's dangerous.'

That made me sit up straight. 'She said what?'

'She doesn't want me here as much, says I should spend more time with her and Dad.'

'Oh, does she now? Well, I'll talk to your dad about that. You are perfectly safe here. If I thought you weren't, there is no way I would have you here.'

'Well, maybe if I had a phone, I'd be safer.'

Well, you clever little rascal, I thought, but inside I was fuming at Pamela.

How dare she put thoughts like that into his head. He

wasn't her child. And Daniel, was he not sticking up for me? Did he not see that I was already in a delicate frame of mind? The last thing I needed was to have someone contesting how much time I should spend with my own son, the most precious thing in my life.

I texted Daniel later that night.

We need to talk. Ben has told me a thing or two that I am not happy about.

When I went to bed, I no longer felt the fear I'd had after leaving the swimming pool. I was overcome by anger at what Pamela had said.

22

DANIEL

I had a feeling what Pamela had said to Ben was going to get back to Nicole and was not going to go down well. So when I got the text from Nicole that she wasn't happy with something Ben had told her, I wasn't too surprised.

Pamela was picking Ben up after school, so I wasn't due to see Nicole that day. I gave her a call at lunchtime instead.

'What has Pamela been saying to Ben about staying with me?' Nicole asked.

'We're all worried, Nicole. It's just a temporary thing until we get everything straightened out.'

'Like the person or persons who are stalking me? Is that part of the straightening out?'

'We don't know what's going on there, Nicole, but you know I support you a hundred percent.'

'That's what I would have thought, Daniel, but I am having to revise that opinion lately. I don't want people taking sides, but yes, you do have to support me. This is a very difficult time, and I feel quite scared.'

I hesitated. This was a delicate balancing act. We had to keep Ben safe though.

'Nicole, if *you* are scared, how do you think Ben feels? Kids pick up on fear intuitively. He said he was worried about what happened in the zoo, but he said it was just about the person losing the money. However, it shows it's playing on his mind.'

'Well, it's playing on my mind too. I need the security of a family and support right now, and not be turned into some sort of pariah.'

'I'll talk to Pamela. To be honest, I thought she went a bit far myself.' I didn't want to say that because there wasn't exactly an ocean of love between Nicole and Pamela, but I felt I had to say something to show Nicole that it had bothered me.

We left the conversation there, but I was even more determined to get to the bottom of the Pablo story. He was due over to Nicole's later that night and was supposedly going to the gym beforehand. I figured that would be an opportunity to check up on him again. Going to the gym appeared to be a cover story for him.

Hidden in my usual shop doorway, I watched Pablo leave the school, light up his cigarette, walk past me on the other side, and look around before turning into the street with the apartments. The same routine as the last two times.

I waited at the bottom of the street with the apartments, not wanting to get caught near the apartment. Sure enough, shortly afterwards, I heard people speaking Spanish approach, and I quickly crossed to the other side of the main road, where I hid. I watched as the three men entered the same internet café I had seen them in before.

They spent about an hour in the café before exiting and chatting outside. I then saw Pablo hug the other two before they returned to the street their apartment was on. Pablo walked away from me, in a direction heading out of town, presumably on his way to Nicole.

As I watched him, I knew I couldn't let the mystery remain just that. It was time to try to find out what was going on with him.

I followed him, knowing that if I really wanted to push the issue with him, there was only one choice. I had to confront him.

How would he react? If he really was up to something dodgy, something that had to be covered up – perhaps a criminal scheme – then I was going to be in the way. That left the question of how well I knew the man. The answer to that was I only knew what had been presented to me.

Outwardly, he seemed like a good guy, genuine and humane – warm even. But that was what he showed to the world. A line from Shakespeare, one of the few I remembered from school, came back to me: 'There's no art / to find the mind's construction in the face'. We don't know what's going on with people until we really get to know them. I didn't know Pablo, but I was going to have to take a chance.

I quickened my pace and started catching up to him. There was no real way of disguising why I was here. I couldn't turn this meeting into some casual coincidence. Nearing him, I took a deep breath.

'Hey, Pablo,' I called to him when I was near enough. He turned, and I saw a look of surprise flash across his features.

'Daniel,' he said, regaining his composure and coming over to shake my hand, 'I don't see you around here before.'

'No, you haven't, and I've got to be honest, there's a reason you're seeing me here today.'

The surprise had disappeared and was replaced with a serious look. 'What's that?'

'Let's walk,' I said, gesturing ahead of us. Whatever I had

to say, I felt it was better that we weren't standing there facing each other, like we were shaping up for a confrontation.

We walked in silence for a few minutes. I could sense he was waiting for me to say something.

'So, Pablo, I suppose Nicole has told you about the strange things that have been happening to her recently.'

'Yes, she have. Pretty bad, no. I'm angry about it. I love to get whoever it is, but I try not to say that to Nicole. She get more worried.' He looked earnestly at me as he said that.

'Well, I've been worrying, I mean we all have about it, and really trying to figure out what's going on. We can't do much until we know, isn't that right?'

'Sure it is.'

'So Nicole told me that you and your family had some problems and that actually you are not Spanish, but from Guatemala.'

Pablo stopped and stared at me. 'She told you that?'

'Of course she did. I'm her ex-husband, and we have a child together. She's going to tell me everything that might affect our family.'

'How my business affect your family?' Pablo faced me. For the first time that evening, I felt a real tremor of fear. I knew this chat had the potential to turn nasty – just how nasty I wasn't sure.

'Nicole is nervous at the moment,' I said, to reduce the tension. 'She needs to be certain about what's going on around her, and, well, your past came as something of a surprise.'

'It's something between me and her,' he said sharply.

'I know it is, but let me finish what I have to say. And please understand that anything I do say is because I want to be sure Nicole and Ben are safe. You would do the same for someone you love, wouldn't you?'

I saw his posture relax a little when I said that.

'Maybe, yeah.'

He said nothing for a minute. It was the longest minute of my life, and I was very conscious of how the two of us standing there facing each other might look to other people. Finally, he reached over and placed a hand on my arm, indicating we should start walking again.

He seemed more relaxed, so I decided to push it a little more. 'I know that you've been telling Nicole you're going to the gym, but you're not really, are you?'

'How do you know that?'

'I had to check, to see what was really going on. I saw you with the other guys.'

Pablo stopped and tensed up again. He looked right at me. After a while he said, 'Okay, I see you are doing this for your family, so I will tell you something.'

We started walking again, and Pablo continued.

'What you said is true. Okay, I was not telling Nicole all the truth, but I was doing that to protect her. My family is in a dangerous situation. These people after my brother, they won't stop. The truth is, those people you see me with, that's my brother and his friend. They are here, and it is very important nobody knows that.'

'I understand,' I said, but my mind was whirring with possibilities. This was a serious situation.

'My brother is getting his new identity now. Soon he will move to another country. I won't say where, but it is better the two of us aren't together.'

'Okay, I see why you were being secretive, but you have to tell Nicole. It's not safe for her and Ben. How do we know these people don't already know where you are?'

'These things that have happened to Nicole, that's not the way these people work. They are killers. They don't play games.'

'That's exactly what bothers me. They are killers. How do you think that makes me feel as a father?'

'I know, because I saw my own father suffer. This thing has been the worst for my family. We are broken up, all over the world, but we are alive. Others are not so lucky. Soon my brother will be gone. Then we will be safe again.'

'And in the meantime what am I to do? Are you at least going to tell Nicole?'

'I will tell her when I think it is safe to. There's a chance she might react badly, do the wrong thing, maybe talk to the police. That would be dangerous for everyone.'

'I'm going to have to think about all this. The safety of my family is my first priority.'

After that I left. I was quite worked up.

Pablo didn't seem to be taking my concerns seriously enough. If he really cared about Nicole, he should tell her and then leave her be until his brother was gone. But if he wasn't going to tell Nicole, then maybe I should.

If Pablo didn't speak up, I would have to seriously consider keeping Ben with me full time, no matter how Nicole felt about it.

23

NICOLE

Ben was still being difficult, but I was determined to just ride his behaviour out. He kept going on about the other kids with phones, but no way was I giving ground on that one.

Pablo came over later that night, and Ben softened a bit when he saw him. They spoke a little Spanish together and then watched a replay of *SpongeBob* with Spanish subtitles. Ben was able to recognise some of the words, and the whole thing kept him entertained for the time he was watching it and then afterwards, when he tested his Spanish and I showed how proud I was.

Just so there wasn't any bad feeling between us, I let him take my phone to bed for a while so he could go on Duolingo and check out some new words. I felt safer once again, having Pablo there with me.

In bed, I told him about the swimming pool incident.

'You think it was kids messing or maybe that person who stalk you again?'

'I don't know. It's hard to think straight anymore. I really don't know what's going on some of the time. You ever get that feeling?'

Pablo smiled and shook his head. 'All the time, my love. All the time.'

The next day I got an email from Alan. He wanted to see me on Saturday. He was ready to disclose what he had been holding back. My dilemma was, should I tell Dorothy, or should I just go ahead and see him myself. I had the keys. It would just be a question of getting in, having the session, and getting out.

My instinct was to go ahead without telling her. I had a nagging feeling that she was going to forbid me. Dorothy had a country house she went to at weekends, so she wouldn't be at the office. If she felt I wasn't in a good frame of mind, she might say no. She had raised those concerns plenty of times already. I had also been avoiding her since my car had gone on fire. I was getting tired of the wary looks she was throwing in my direction. Despite everything that had been happening to me, I felt that I was still rational enough to see Alan. The prospect of finally getting to the bottom of Alan's trauma was a strong motivator. I didn't want to jeopardise his progress.

It was still early in the week, so I didn't have to make an immediate decision. I wasn't one who liked to put things off, but I felt that if I left it much closer to the Saturday to tell Dorothy, then she would find it harder to turn me down. It would be too short notice to cancel Alan's appointment, and she was always telling me we had to be careful with our clients. Disappointment or sudden changes in schedule could have a strong negative impact. I felt a bit cynical taking this ploy, but I really wanted the meeting to go ahead.

I had a full schedule of clients for the day, so it passed quickly. There was a little time for write-ups at the end, and I was glad of the time to collect my thoughts. As usual, after any busy day, as soon as the clients had gone, I felt exhaustion kick in. I had to give each client my full attention, and at the same time as they talked, I had to try to figure out the best way forward. Momentum was key, and the clients needed to feel that I was giving them a roadmap towards some sort of resolution. That might just be an acceptance of their pain rather than any major change, but it must be a resolution of sorts.

This search for solutions played on my mind during my clients' sessions. The events of the recent past had unsettled me hugely, and it made the process of finding them more difficult. After all that had happened, I had begun to doubt my own judgement, and in a one-to-one therapeutic relationship where my judgement was key... well, that was both unnerving and exhausting.

I left work after six in the replacement car the insurance company had given me. I was looking forward to getting home and chilling out for the evening. Fatigue had gripped me hard, so I turned up the volume on the radio to stop myself from dozing off on the drive home. I took my usual route and thought I spotted a blue car a few cars behind that was taking the same turns as me.

That's just a coincidence, I thought as my mind flicked nervously back to the white car that had followed me and tried to push me into traffic. *Plenty of people take these shortcuts, given the way traffic is these days.*

But the blue car kept on showing up, and as traffic thinned, it was getting closer and closer to me. Now my nerves were really starting to hit. My heart beat faster, and my grip on the steering wheel was so tight, my knuckles were turning white.

Another turn and the same blue car appeared in my rearview mirror. It was right behind me now.

A plan started to formulate quickly in my mind. If this was the same person, then it would make for perfect evidence if I could get them to follow me to the police station. The problem was we would have that big intersection to cross. If the lights were against me, I was in trouble again.

I reached for my phone. This time I was calling the Gardai and wasn't getting out of my car until they came.

Then a strange thing happened.

The car started flashing their lights at me, and I was sure I could see the driver waving. Looking closer at the driver, I saw they weren't dressed in dark clothing. It was a man as far as I could make out. Looking closer, I could see it was someone I recognised.

Next thing, the car pulled up alongside me, and the person rolled down the window. It was Pete, and he was gesturing for me to pull over. Farther up the road was a small layby, and I pulled in there. Pete pulled in behind me and jumped from his car to run up beside my window.

I put it down.

'Hi, Nicole. Listen, sorry for coming up on you like that. I wanted to talk and didn't have your number. I was going to wait for you after work, but I saw you pulling out, so I followed you.'

'Pete, what the hell...?' I said. 'You just gave me the fright of my life. What were you thinking? You could have called my work.'

He ran a hand through his hair. He looked distinctly more middle-aged than when I had last seen him, thinner on top and thicker around the waist. He still had the same deep, sorrowful eyes that so many women had fallen for in his younger days. We'd all thought of him as some poetic, romantic figure, and he'd been quite happy to play the part.

'Yeah, I'm sorry,' Pete said. 'I wasn't sure what to do. All I knew was that I needed to talk to you, somewhere in private, and as I say, I don't have your number anymore.'

He was leaning in my car window. I wasn't sure what he was going to come out with next, so I stayed put.

'I guess Daniel probably spoke to you,' he said, his eyes looking even more sorrowful than before.

'Yes, he did.'

'I'm sorry, Nicole. It's been on my conscience forever. When I heard you guys had split, well, it took me time, but I finally got the courage to talk to Daniel.'

'And you didn't think to talk to me first?' I said sharply. I was still annoyed with him. It was all well and good to make a clean breast of things for his sake, but he must have known that speaking to my ex would make things difficult for me.

'Well, I thought, seeing as it was all over between you, what was the harm?'

'Some of it is all over between us, but a lot of it is not. We have a son together, remember?'

'I know. I should have thought more before I went to Daniel, but I had to get it off my chest.'

'Well, I'm glad you managed to do that much. Meanwhile, I'm left to deal with the fallout... But as it happens, I have bigger fish to fry at the moment, so we'll leave it there. And kindly don't try to make contact with me again.'

I put my window up and took off at speed. Pete staggered back as I did, almost losing his balance. I checked in my rearview mirror though and saw he was okay, standing at the side of the road, looking more sorrowful than ever.

My heart raced as I drove home, but at the same time I felt relief. I hadn't been in danger.

Straight after that I had another thought. *What is happening to my life? I feel threatened all the time. It's crazy that I feel relieved when it's not someone trying to harm me.*

I decided I had to get my life back whatever it took.

24

DANIEL

'Ben was being snotty with me again,' Pamela whispered when I arrived home. I was tired after a long day at the shop and was hoping to flake out on the couch after dinner.

'Oh, how?' I could see she was quite riled up.

'I asked him about his homework, and he snapped at me, saying something about I shouldn't think I know everything just because I study. Then he stormed off to his room.'

'Okay, I'll talk to him. That's no way to talk to you.'

I tapped lightly on Ben's bedroom door and, hearing no response, pushed it open. He was lying on his bed, staring up at the ceiling. I went over and sat on the bed and pushed his hair back from his face. He shook his head in response so the hair fell over his eyes again.

'What was up between yourself and Pamela? She said you snapped at her when she asked about homework.'

'No, I didn't. It's just not any of her business. Who is she to me?'

'She's a person who looks after you and cares about you.'

'My mum does that, and Pamela wants to keep me away

from her.' He turned away to face the wall after he said that. I rubbed his shoulder and back.

'It's not like that, Ben. It's just that... sometimes people go through difficulties, and it's maybe not the best time to be around them. It's better to give them time on their own.'

'That's not how I feel,' he muttered to the wall. 'If my mum is having what you call a difficulty, then I want to be with her.'

'That's very good of you, Ben, to say that. Your mum would be very proud.'

'I want to be with her is all, and not with that other woman.' He turned and nodded in the direction of the living room before facing the wall again. I decided there and then that we had to try to get to the bottom of whatever was going on as quickly as we could. If part of that process meant telling Nicole the whole truth about Pablo, well, I wasn't going to hold back.

I went for a walk later that evening and gave her a call. It had to be out of earshot of both Pamela and Ben.

'Hey,' I said when she answered, trying to at least start off with a light tone.

'Everything okay?' She sounded concerned.

'Yeah, of course. Ben was a little out of sorts, nothing major, but I thought I should give you a call and fill you in.'

'That's good of you. I'm a bit worried about him alright. He was a bit short with me and didn't seem too happy.'

'He's not too happy, and who could blame him. There's a lot of uncertainty, I guess... actually, there's something I need to tell you. I mean, it's something I said I wouldn't, but it's important, particularly with Ben acting up.'

'Yeah? What is it? Pablo is due over any minute.'

'Yeah, well, it kind of concerns Pablo.'

'In what way?'

'To cut to the chase... erm, I've been keeping an eye on him.'

'You what?' Nicole's tone increased a couple of octaves.

'Yeah, there's no way of dressing it up or gilding the lily or whatever that expression is. I followed him for a couple of days. I had to see if he was up to anything dodgy after we discovered that he's in Ireland under a false identity.'

'You followed him without telling me?' Nicole said slowly.

'I did, because if I'd told you before I had, how would you have reacted? You would have tried to stop me. And this is the point I'm trying to make... it's just as well I did, because I found something out that is quite important.'

There was a pause. Then Nicole asked, 'What was that?'

'His brother is here, living in an apartment in the city centre, not far from where Pablo teaches.'

'How do you know it's his brother?' Nicole's tone had picked up again.

'Because I saw him with a man twice, so I just went up when Pablo was alone and asked him.'

'Oh my God, Daniel, what the hell are you doing? Pablo is my new partner, and you are spying on him.'

Her reaction threw me. I had expected her to understand I was doing this for her. 'But if I hadn't, you wouldn't have known. Don't you get the importance of that? If his brother is here, then the people who are looking for him might be here as well, or could be soon if they track him down. That's dangerous, Nicole, for both you and Ben.'

Another pause. 'I don't know what to say, Daniel. This feels so intrusive, but I understand what you're telling me. I see it's important, but where does that leave me? Where does it leave Pablo?'

'I don't know, Nicole, but I had to tell you.'

We left the conversation there. I didn't like finishing on a bad note, but it was the truth. What was she going to do about Pablo? Nicole had to make that decision for herself. Meanwhile, I had to make my own decisions regarding Ben.

Pamela wasn't too helpful when I returned.

'I've been thinking,' she said, 'that you're probably right in what you said before, that Ben is acting up because of what's going on. That's only going to get worse if we let him stay with Nicole. You have to show leadership here and tell Nicole that it's not suitable to have him over there.'

'I was just talking to Nicole about the whole thing.'

I didn't mention the new information I had about Pablo. That would just reinforce Pamela's negative opinion. I was beginning to wonder if Pamela had another agenda anyway. She'd never seemed that fond of Nicole, like she was jealous of my past with her. Maybe she was using this as an excuse to get back at her.

'And?' Pamela had raised both eyebrows in expectation of my response.

'And, well, she is aware, and she is also concerned, but it's something she and I need to work out together.'

'Oh, so I don't count, do I? Well, it's good to know where I stand.'

Pamela lurched up off the couch and walked briskly from the room.

I was left standing there, my phone still in my hand. I wasn't sure where all this was going. I wasn't sure about an awful lot of things.

25

NICOLE

Pablo came over shortly after Daniel's call. I was still in a state of shock and confusion. What should I say to him?

Nothing felt like the most appropriate response for the moment. I couldn't tell him that Daniel had told me about his brother. I would have to say it eventually if Pablo didn't, but I hoped he would.

Could I trust him? That was the main question I asked myself.

If he was prepared to keep secrets from me, then what else was he hiding?

That thought really distressed me. Having him around had made me feel secure; now, with his new secret, the carpet had been well and truly pulled from under my feet. Whom could I trust now? Even with Daniel, I knew that Pamela was pulling his strings a little, and I was sure he had conflicted loyalties.

Tomorrow was Friday, and I was due to meet Alan on Saturday, so I had to try to shake all these misgivings and concentrate on my work. With the rest of my life in such a mess, it was important to me that I get at least one part right. I wanted to prove to myself that I could still do my job well. Alan was, I hoped, going to provide me with the opportunity to show I could do that.

As for Dorothy, I had decided how I would approach her.

The next day, I arranged to see her late in the afternoon. Walking into her office, I felt butterflies in my stomach. I stood in front of her desk and swallowed before I spoke.

'Dorothy, you remember my client Alan I spoke to you about before?'

'Of course I do,' she replied irritably.

'Well, I just got an email from him, and he wants to see me urgently. He really wants to come in tomorrow morning.'

'I thought we discussed this already, and we questioned whether you were in the right frame of mind to see somebody when the building is so quiet?'

'I know, but we have to put the client first. There's something he really needs to get off his chest, and if he feels the need to do that when there's nobody around, well, I have to accommodate that.'

'So you are going against my advice?' Dorothy looked at me like I was an annoying insect that refused to go away.

'I appreciate your advice very much, but in this case, I feel it's in the best interest of the client to see him tomorrow. He really needs to disclose something. If holding onto it is proving too much for him, then I have to respect that.'

'You know I can't be here on Saturday.' She was still giving me a look like she wished I would just vaporize.

'I know, and I don't want to cause you any undue stress, but, as I said, it is in the best interest of the client.'

I turned to leave then, even though my leaving felt a little abrupt and rude. But if I stayed any longer, Dorothy would keep trying to dissuade me. I could feel her eyes bore into my back as I walked out, but I kept going. I had to prove I was fine, and if angering Dorothy was what it took, then I was willing to tolerate it.

That night I was all alone. Pablo wasn't coming over, and I was glad for the space. I was still figuring out how best to deal with the new information Daniel had given me about Pablo.

On Saturday morning I was up early. That gave me plenty of time to prepare for my meeting with Alan. I made a quick breakfast of fresh fruit and granola and had a shot of espresso. Feeling fresh and awake, I drove through the relatively quiet weekend streets, listening to classical music on Lyric FM, doing my best to get into a calm state and clear my mind before meeting him.

He was due at 10am, and I reached the offices by 9am. I entered through the downstairs door and knocked off the alarm. Then I went to the kitchen and threw the kettle on to make tea.

After a cuppa and feeling refreshed and ready for the day, I went into my office and pulled out Alan's file. Taking a look through it, I could see the difficulty and dysfunction that had followed him through his life. He had done well to get where he was, with all the outward appearance of success, but I knew how he felt, thinking that his life was a sham, merely covering up the pain that he carried inside.

I had lived a lot of my own life exactly like that. I was a survivor too, putting on a brave face for the world, hiding my vulnerability. I had no doubt that was a large part of why Daniel and I had split. My vulnerability had come to the fore when I was stalked by Gary. My life had suddenly become a maelstrom of confused emotions, and Daniel had got the brunt of it.

Having checked through Alan's file and feeling that I had a good grasp on his background, I waited, allowing the peace of the quiet, old building to suffuse me. It was a huge and solid structure, built back when the country was still in

English hands. Much of Dublin city's architecture had come from that time, and sitting in such a grand building, my thoughts drifted to the life of whatever aristocrats might have once lorded over the place. They would have had a team of servants building fires, cooking, serving, looking after their children.

What a strange life, I thought, *living in comfort while on the other side of the city, we had some of the worst slums in Europe.*

I checked the digital clock on the mantelpiece and saw it was 9.50am. Alan was due in ten minutes. I had to admit that I felt a little nervous at the prospect of the meeting. At the same time, I was confident I could handle whatever it was he wanted to disclose. So much had been disclosed to me during my career as a counsellor. Sometimes I had struggled to keep the professional mask intact when I'd listened to stories of childhood abuse, but I knew how important it was to keep that calm, attentive demeanour. It gave the client the confidence and space to continue, giving them the feeling that they finally had a safe place to share their burden.

10am hit, and I listened out for the doorbell. It dawned on me that Alan might well lose his nerve and not turn up. That was sometimes the case when clients had something major to disclose. Once the nerve was lost, I often found it hard to reel them back in again. They would sometimes start making excuses, saying that they're feeling a lot better, and maybe it was time to give counselling a break. I hoped that wouldn't be the case with Alan. He seemed like he was on the cusp of a real breakthrough. But it was hard for a young man like him to come to sessions under his own steam, so I really wanted it to work for him.

At 10.10am I went to his file and searched for his contact number. Tapping it into my phone, I waited for an answer. The phone went to voicemail.

Bad sign.

I left a message, in the hope he might have forgotten or got the times wrong, but I was starting to suspect the worst. He was not contactable, and that was probably the way he wanted it.

So I had to decide how long I was going to give him. Being in the huge building alone was starting to unsettle me. Maybe I had made a mistake going against Dorothy's advice. I had been stubborn and insistent because I believed it was the right thing to do for Alan. Now he was letting me down, and thoughts of all the strange things that had happened to me started coming back.

Somebody was tracking my movements. The incident with the car in traffic, the swimming pool – all of it pointed to somebody knowing when I would be alone and choosing the right moment to frighten me. What if they had seen me leave my house early this morning and followed me to what would be a deserted building? Just my rental car was parked outside. This would be the perfect time to do something really nasty.

I had to get out, even if it meant leaving Alan in the lurch. It was 10.15am, and I had given him enough time. I had to think about myself.

These thoughts were flooding my mind as I snatched my bag and the bunch of keys I had left on my desk. I would lock up and go.

My phone was in my bag. Such was my state of worry that I even felt like calling Pablo, just to hear a familiar voice.

I was just closing the door to my office, ready to dash up the hall and out the main door, when I heard a sound outside. Stopping, my heart already pounding in my chest, I listened.

There it was again, like something rubbing on the door. Then another sound, something human, or almost human, a gurgling sound, followed by what sounded like a long, low moan.

Oh God, I heard myself say. *What's that?*

'Hello?' I shouted at the door. 'Is there somebody out there?'

Another long moan and that sound of something brushing on the door. I reached for my phone and called Pablo. Voicemail.

Damn it, he was probably still in bed. I tried Daniel next. Voicemail too.

The moan outside got louder. I went to the door and pressed my eye against the glass spyhole. There, I could see the top of a head of hair. It was brown and wavy, just like Alan's. Was he there? What was wrong with him?

Left with no choice, I eased the big wooden door open slowly, peering through it as I did. Alan was standing but hunched over. I yanked the door open and reached out to help him in, but as I did, he collapsed in my arms. I felt something wet and sticky against my skin. Looking down, I saw my hands were covered in blood.

'Oh my God,' I said and tried to hold him up, but he was a dead weight and leaning into me. An eerie gurgling sound came from his throat. I caught a glimpse of his face. It was a deathly grey-white. His eyes were almost fully closed, and his mouth hung open.

Then he leaned in more, his full weight against my arms, pushing me back. I screamed and tried to get out of the way, while at the same time reaching out to stop his fall. He was too big and heavy for me, and the forward momentum kept him coming. All I could do was lurch to the side.

He fell heavily to the floor, a gasp of air rushing from his lungs. And then he just lay there, motionless.

I saw one final spasm run through his body before every part of him just folded to the ground, unmoving.

I backed down the hall, wanting nothing more than to

run screaming from the building, but he was there. My client Alan was lying dead in the hallway.

I looked down at my clothes, at the fresh, lime-coloured dress I had put on that morning. My hands and the dress were covered in Alan's blood.

I reached unthinking into my bag, which was hanging off one arm, and pulled out my phone.

Robotically, I dialled the emergency services number. I could hear my own voice faintly as I spoke into the phone.

'Something terrible has happened. There's a man lying on the floor. I think he's dead.'

26

DANIEL

The shop was quiet, but that was nothing unusual for a Saturday morning. It was only 10.30am. The city centre was slowly coming to life. Street-cleaning machines buzzed past the door, spraying jets of water. Lorries and vans passed up and down the street, doing morning deliveries. The occasional knots of revellers staggered past. Some of the early houses did a steady trade for those who wanted the night to go on forever. Sometimes I'd see young men in tuxes and women in long, flowy dresses and heels do battle with the morning light, the memories of their night still etched on their faces. The women's false tans and smeared mascara gave them a theatrical appearance.

A couple of early morning tourists wandered into the shop, dressed in those see-through rain macs that were a giveaway for identifying continental Europeans and Americans who visited Ireland. No doubt they had heard about the infamous rain on these shores, and no matter how fine the day was looking, they were taking no chances. I nodded in greeting to them and left them to browse.

My phone was on the small table where I had the cash

register. From where I was standing, I could hear it move and vibrate.

It's probably Pamela with some question about Ben's schedule, I thought. *I'll call back in a minute.*

But as soon as the phone stopped vibrating, it started up again.

That's odd, I thought. *Must be something more urgent.*

I saw one of the tourists look over in the direction of the phone. I smiled and nodded as I walked quickly towards it. Picking it up, I could see it was Nicole calling.

At first, I found it hard to make out what Nicole was saying, she was speaking so quickly.

'Okay, calm down. Calm down,' I said, trying to keep my own voice calm and even. The two tourists were still looking around the shop. I moved to the back so I'd be slightly out of earshot.

'What's happening? Try to tell me slowly.'

'It's Alan. He's dead. I'm at the police station. The one near my work. They think I might have killed him. They're questioning me.'

'Who?' My mind raced through the possibilities. Alan... I remember she had told me about him, but who was it?

'Where did it happen? Who is Alan?' I asked desperately.

'The new client. The guy I told you about.' Nicole was crying. She mumbled something, but I couldn't hear through the sobs.

'Okay, give me a minute. I'm going to have to close up here. I'll be there as quick as I can.'

When I put the phone down, I tried desperately to understand what she had just said. None of it made sense, yet she had told me, clear as day, that one of her clients had been murdered, and they were holding her as a suspect. The dead client was Alan. I remembered now how she had mentioned a young man who'd reminded her a bit of Gary. Now he was dead. None of it made sense. All I knew was I had to help her, and fast.

Smiling as best I could, I told the tourists I had to close up for an hour or two but would be back. They looked a little confused as they headed out into the street, which was starting to get busy with shoppers. I pulled the shutter down and ran to my car.

After pulling out into the traffic, I tried to concentrate on the road ahead, but all I could hear was Nicole's voice telling me that this young guy Alan was dead. How could that have happened? How could the police even think that Nicole was involved?

Nicole? Killing someone? My ex who had done nothing but help people for as long as I knew her. But then a disquieting thought came to me. So many strange things had been happening around Nicole, yet nobody had appeared on the radar as a suspect. Was there really somebody after her, or was this some dangerous fantasy world that she had got lost in?

I pushed all such thoughts out of my mind as I parked at the station and walked through the wooden double doors of the police station. I could feel the blood drain from my face as I went. I approached the counter, and a pleasant, young, female Garda took my name and details and asked me to wait.

Some minutes later, the same Garda used a swipe card to unlock another wooden door that led into the station proper. Inside were a series of interview rooms, and Nicole was sitting in one of them on one side of a wooden table. On the other side sat a Garda with thinning hair and a thin, bony face.

'Next of kin?' the Garda asked as I walked in.

'Yes, I'm her ex-husband.'

'Well, Nicole has been involved in a serious incident, and we needed to get some details, but she is free to go for now.'

I noted the 'for now' but said nothing. Nicole stood shakily, and I took her elbow to lead her from the room. The young female Garda swiped the big door again, and we walked through the foyer and out of the station, into the morning light.

Neither of us spoke until we got to my car.

'What happened?' I asked.

Nicole shook her head, looking at the ground. Her shoulders were shaking. She had obviously been crying. She was wearing a grey tracksuit that I hadn't seen before.

'They gave me this,' she said, pulling at the tracksuit. 'They kept my dress because there was blood on it. They wanted to keep it as evidence.' Her shoulders kept shaking. I put my arms around her and held her. She sobbed quietly, shaking all the time.

'My car is back at work. I need to go there,' she said eventually. 'They brought me here in a police car, said I wouldn't be allowed to drive. It was horrible, Daniel, horrible. He's dead.'

I opened the passenger door of my car, and Nicole climbed in unsteadily. Once we were moving, she started to talk.

'It was Alan. Poor Alan. I don't know what happened. I was waiting for him. Then he was at the door... and the blood, so much blood. All over my dress. It was horrible.'

'How did he die?' I had to know. It was all too confusing.

'They say he was stabbed. A big knife. They can't be completely sure till after the post-mortem, but that's what they think. The paramedics tried to save him. Nothing they could do. They asked me so many questions, but I don't know. I just don't know. I'm sorry I called you. I couldn't call Pablo, not with his past. I was afraid they'd check his identity. I'm sorry.'

'It's okay. I understand. It's better you called me.' I reached across to rub her shoulder.

'I'll call Pablo now. I need him with me today. I can't think.'

We arrived at her workplace. There was red tape all around the door and the car park. Nicole's car was off to the side. There were still Gardaí there; some were hunkered down in the car park, sifting through the gravel.

She walked gingerly to her car, opened the door slowly and peered inside, like she was expecting someone or something to be in there. I walked over to stand beside her.

'Are you okay to drive? You could leave the car here, and I'll bring you home.'

'Oh, no. Then it would be here for the whole weekend.' She gestured broadly at her workplace, which had now become a crime scene. I could see exactly where she was coming from. The whole place represented danger now.

'Okay, I'll drive behind you. If you feel like stopping any time, do.'

We drove at what felt to me like a funereal pace back to her house. Once we got there, I helped her in and put the kettle on. Nicole threw herself onto the couch and lay there, staring up at the ceiling. Her breathing was slow and sounded laboured.

I brought her a mug of tea and some biscuits.

'Here, get these into you. The sugar will do you good.'

She sat up straight and took some sips from the tea, nibbled at a biscuit, but her eyes were glassy, and she seemed a million miles away.

'You should call Pablo,' I suggested.

'Of course,' she said, her voice flat. She lifted her phone and called him.

27

NICOLE

At the police station, I had gone into a trance-like state. They'd offered me some spare clothes because mine were covered in blood. Alan's blood. My client's blood.

I was having real difficulty taking that in.

In my mind I went through the events of the morning again and again. That was just what the Garda who was interviewing me had wanted me to do. That just reinforced what had happened.

'I'd been waiting for Alan, my client, and he didn't show up on time. And then he did show up, but he was dying, and then he fell on top of me, and I screamed and I screamed, and then I called emergency services.'

I repeated the same story. Over and over.

The Garda asked me about Alan. I told him what I knew – his history, his abuse, the severe problems at home that had put him in foster care and then a care home. Client confidentiality went out the window when a client died. We only kept it as long as we believed there was no danger to the client or that they weren't a danger to anyone else. Well, the danger to

Alan had been proven, but now it was well and truly past. Too late for Alan.

It had been comforting to see Daniel. His presence had somehow brought me back into the world, the world that had changed forever at about ten fifteen that morning. It had been a surprise to see other people walking around on the streets, in their cars. They'd looked unreal. Did they know what had just happened?

Seeing my workplace with Gardai crawling all over it and the red tape had made me freeze again. Only Daniel's presence and words had pushed me back into robotic action. I could drive home, just about. My hands and feet had operated independently of my brain on the way home. They did all the things they'd been doing for years, while I was a million miles away.

At home, I'd called Pablo. Over the phone I'd told him something terrible had happened, no details. Daniel told me he'd wait until Pablo showed up before leaving.

I told Daniel I needed a couple of minutes alone. I flicked my computer on to see if there was any news of the incident. Nothing yet. I sipped tea that Daniel had made for me and stared out my front window, the radio crackling in the background.

When Pablo arrived, Daniel left, and I recalled the events as best I could. Pablo listened with an open mouth, sitting on the couch beside me, holding my hand. Every now and then he said, 'No,' or something in Spanish. His tanned face looked paler than I had ever seen it before.

'This is the worst,' he said as I finished. 'That is so hard for you. Your client. Who could do something like that?'

That was the question I had been trying to avoid, but the one that kept rearing up. Who would do something like that? Who would kill a young man in cold blood, and why? I had no answer.

Pablo stayed with me all day. It was a Saturday, and through the window, I could see the families going about their business – shopping, trips out, kids playing, all the normal stuff – and here I was, in a bubble of shock.

Dorothy called me later. My phone lit up, and I saw her name scrolled across the screen. My hand shook as I answered.

'What happened?' she asked. 'The police have been on to me. I'm on my way back.'

I told her as much as I could. The Gardai wanted her there so they could have a look inside the building, see if there were any clues. As she told me that, I was acutely aware that I had been the only person inside the building that morning. Were they going to search my office, look for clues as to what I had been doing?

The answer I gave myself was of *course they were*. It had been just me, and then Alan showed up, covered in blood, and it was all over the hallway of the building. I was there, nobody else. Of course I was the number one suspect.

Two detectives arrived at my house later in the afternoon. They knocked politely and stood back from the door when I opened it. They were casually dressed, both wearing jeans. One wore a sports jacket, the other a bomber-style jacket.

'My name's Detective Byrne,' the guy in the sports jacket said, 'and that's Detective Peters. We'd like you to come over to the crime scene later on, as you might be able to give us a bit of extra detail we need.'

I think I nodded. The last thing I wanted to do was go back there. As soon as they left, Pablo came over to put an arm around me.

'I go with you, Nicole. It's better I drive,' he said.

'You're very kind, but what about your ID? You don't want anyone asking you questions.'

'It's okay. I'll stay out of the way.'

The idea of going back there filled me with a sickening dread, so I didn't object any more to him coming. I badly needed the support and was grateful for it. I understood why they wanted me there. I was the only witness, and that made me feel very vulnerable indeed.

We pulled into the car park of my offices half an hour later. There was a bit less police activity than before. The two detectives were waiting outside for me. Dorothy was there too, standing beside them. She looked quizzically at me as I got out of the car, as if she was really seeing me for the first time.

Detective Byrne led me to the door, the place where Alan had been and fallen on me. He got me to recount again what had happened and to talk about the physical aspect of it. Where exactly he was standing, how exactly he fell. Did I see an injury then or later?

'I saw no specific injury,' I replied. 'But there was blood everywhere.'

The detective nodded in understanding. I could see activity around the door of my office. There were voices coming from inside. Once I had gone over my story again, the detective told me I was free to go. I had to walk past Dorothy as I left, so I stopped, looking around at the scene, as she was.

'Who would do something like that?' she asked, looking at the spot where Gardaí were combing the ground for clues.

I took a deep breath, intending to say something, although I wasn't sure what, but when I exhaled, nothing came out. I could find no words.

Dorothy was staring at me, however, waiting.

'I'm sorry. I can't speak about it,' I managed. 'It's all been too much.'

She said nothing, but her eyes wandered over my face, then continued on up to look at the building, her business, the place that would soon be on every news broadcast in the country.

The days after went by in a blur. News of the killing got out, and soon there were shots of the beautiful Georgian building splashed everywhere. Shots of Alan's handsome, youthful face also filled the screens, some stories hinting at his troubled past, others just lamenting what a terrible loss it was for a young man who had achieved so much and had so much to look forward to. An active murder investigation was underway, and a Garda spokesman reported that no stone would be unturned until the killer was brought to justice.

I didn't go into work.

I had emailed Dorothy and called in sick. She sent me a curt reply to the effect of it was best if I didn't come in and to take some leave. That left me at home with not a whole lot to do except to ruminate. Pablo spent as much time with me as he could. That helped. We went for walks and coffees, but I never felt present. My mind was always at the scene, with Alan, trying to roll the clock back, to make like it hadn't happened. Then my therapist voice would kick in, and I knew it had happened, and I had to face it somehow.

I was called down to the Garda station again. This time I brought a solicitor with me. I had been in touch with a legal firm that we sometimes used for our counselling practice, and they'd advised me to get legal representation. I had to make a formal statement and sign it, so the solicitor read carefully through it first.

I wasn't sure where I was on the spectrum of 'people of interest' to the Gardaí, but I figured I must be pretty high up. They were keeping their cards close to their chest, saying they were following 'a number of lines of enquiry'. The murder weapon had not yet been found, but the evidence pointed to a large knife having been used. The official state pathologist report had not been signed off yet. There would be no funeral until that was completed.

I wondered, when the time for the funeral came, who would be there. Did Alan have anyone close left in his life? He had mentioned siblings who had left for Australia. I supposed they would be informed and return.

Daniel called over a couple of evenings when Pablo wasn't around, just to keep me company. It was considered best that Ben didn't stay with me right now, and for once I was in agreement. I was in no fit state to look after anyone.

The second evening Daniel was there, he asked me if I had any idea who might have killed Alan.

'No, I can honestly say I don't,' I replied. 'Who would do such a thing? It's pure evil.'

'Have you ever considered he may have had connections you didn't know about?'

'Of course, he had a dodgy past, but he seemed to have left that all behind. That's the reason he was coming to me. He wanted to make peace with his past and move on.'

'Just out of curiosity, did Pablo have any thoughts on it?'

That question took me by surprise. 'How do you mean?'

'Well, given what he's been through, maybe he'd have some insight.'

'Not necessarily. This is a different country, different culture... Anyway, I don't like the idea of dragging his name into it.'

'Of course not, but you have to think of every possibility, I suppose.'

'I'm not sure what you mean by that, but I don't think *I* need to think of every possibility. That's what the Gardaí are there for.'

'Of course, of course, I'm just thinking everything through.'

That conversation left me feeling uneasy. I wasn't sure

exactly what Daniel was implying, but I didn't like that he was bringing Pablo into it. But why had all this nasty stuff happened around me? Was Alan's killing connected to the other stuff?

The conclusion I came to was yes, it probably was, but that brought me no closer to knowing who the killer was.

What it did, however, was make me suspicious of everyone. I couldn't think straight. What Daniel had said certainly didn't help. I was already concerned about Pablo and the slow reveal of his past. I needed to trust him, to have someone solid I could lean on, but did I now think of him as someone who might be in some way involved?

I really hoped not, but was there anything I could be certain of anymore?

28

DANIEL

'I'm not going.' Ben was refusing to go to school. I had to go and open the shop. Pamela was going to have to deal with this, and she wasn't happy.

'You need to go to school, Ben,' I said. 'You're not sick. There'll be days when you are sick and you need to take time off.'

'I don't care. I don't feel well, so I'm not going.'

I had to leave to open the shop. Pamela was looking helplessly at me, her arms spread wide.

'Ben, if you go to school today, we'll do something really nice at the weekend. I promise.'

He said nothing for a minute and then, 'I don't want to do anything really nice. I want to stay with my mum.'

We had shielded him as best we could from what had happened at Nicole's work, but with information going round the way it did these days, I couldn't be sure he hadn't picked up on some of it. Although Nicole's name had never been mentioned in the news reports.

'You will be staying with your mum again. It's just for short time you need to stay here.'

'That's what you keep on saying.'

I wasn't going to argue with him about his childish concept of time. It had only been a short while since he'd been staying with us full time.

'If you don't go to school, they'll want to know why,' Pamela said to Ben.

'It's because I don't feel well.'

'You look fine to me,' she said and looked at me for backup.

'I think you're more upset than feeling sick,' I said, deciding to be honest about it. I really had to go and open the shop, so this had to come to a conclusion.

'I am upset, and that makes me feel sick,' Ben said and folded his arms defiantly.

'Okay then, just for today you can stay home, but we'll have to have a good chat about it later.'

I left then, even though Pamela was glaring at me. She was going to be stuck with Ben for the day, and she had lots of assignments to get through, but I had no choice. The shop had to be opened.

After opening up, I started to think everything through. I knew Pamela would lose patience very quickly, staying at home with a confused boy who was being hostile to her. It simply wasn't going to work. I had to try to speed up a resolution with Nicole, and that meant taking action.

Was there anything more in the Pablo story that was still to be revealed? One person I felt might know something about Nicole's state of mind and what was going on at the house was James, her neighbour. He would be witness to the comings and goings at Nicole's, and he had been caught up in those strange incidents early on.

I took a chance and gave him a call. There was no way of dressing things up; I had to cut to the chase.

'James, it's Daniel here. Sorry for calling you out of the

blue, but would you be able to meet for a coffee? I'm worried about Nicole.'

There was a pause on the other end of the line, followed by what sounded like a sigh, before James said, 'Sure. I'm free at 12.30pm, but just for twenty minutes.'

I closed up shop early and met James at a small coffee shop in town. He worked in advertising, and they had offices near the city centre.

He arrived a few minutes after me, grabbed a coffee at the counter and sat down at a small wooden table towards the back of the coffee shop. I had chosen it because it gave us some privacy. The noise from clattering coffee cups and the hiss of the milk steamer gave us more.

'Thanks for coming,' I said. 'Things have been pretty challenging to say the least.'

'I saw on the news. I was pretty sure that was the place Nicole worked.'

'It was. She's in bits of course, but there have been a lot of other things happening too. Like what happened with you, you know... the weird love note and the damage to your car.'

James nodded. I could see he was stiffening up at the memory of it.

'I'm worried, James, to put it mildly, and I was wondering if you can shed any light on what things are like at the house. You must see a lot of comings and goings. I'm keeping Ben away at the moment, and he's really acting up. He wants to get back there, but I'm nervous about it.'

'I don't blame you,' James said, eyeing me warily. 'But where do I come into it? I had that unpleasant incident with Nicole, but I'd rather just forget about it and move on.'

'I understand, but it's just as a former neighbour and, well, a friend of sorts, I thought you might be able to shed a bit of light.'

James looked even more wary. I could sense his increasing agitation. He drank a good gulp of coffee and looked around.

'I don't want to get involved, Daniel. I think it's unfair of you to ask me to more or less spy on your wife. Whatever's going on is between you two.'

'Of course. It's just... I'm in a sticky situation, with Ben and everything. You understand. You've got kids.'

'I do have a child, and I very much keep that between me and my wife. I'm sorry, Daniel, but you are putting me in an awkward position, and I don't appreciate it.' He grabbed his jacket from the back of his chair and left.

There was no point calling after him. All I could do was send him a text saying:

thanks for coming and sorry if I overstepped the mark.

He didn't reply.

That left me to mull things over more when I returned to the shop. I could understand it from James's point of view, but for the sake of safety in the neighbourhood, surely it was not too much to let me know if he had seen anything unusual.

It was clear he was trying to keep as much of a distance as he could from Nicole and, by association, from me. Whatever was happening, *I* was going to have to figure it out. If it came to it, I would have to watch the house myself and, if needed, watch Nicole.

Everything that was going on revolved around her.

29

NICOLE

The Gardaí brought me in again for questioning. I brought my young solicitor, Kieran, in with me, as that was what he had advised.

'You're not being treated as a suspect at this time,' he assured me when we met outside the Garda station. He might only be in his early thirties, but he already had an air of authority about him. I guessed that was to reassure me, the client, he was taking it seriously and that he was someone I could depend on. I appreciated that, but it also made me feel I was treading a fine line between witness and suspect.

The two detectives who had called to my house were waiting in the interview room.

'Nicole, thanks for coming,' Byrne said. Like I had any choice in the matter.

'It's a formality, really,' Peters said, 'just to go through the events of the day again. Sometimes the shock of something as horrific as this can make us forget details.'

I knew that well, how trauma was a very effective memory blocker, but I wasn't going to say it to them.

'Of course, I understand,' I replied and began to recount the events again.

Whatever trauma I had experienced, the memory of what had happened after I first heard Alan moaning outside would stay with me forever. No fear of forgetting it. It had kept me awake every night since, and when I did finally get to sleep, I would wake again with a start and often a shout. I kept seeing some terrible, indefinable shape falling sharply towards me.

'So the noises at the door were the first indication you had that someone was out there,' Byrne said.

'Yes, someone or something. I wasn't sure.'

'Of course, but it was a noise that attracted your attention.'

'Yes, I was just getting ready to go because I thought he wasn't coming.'

'Was he usually punctual?' Peters asked.

'The couple of times he had come to me, yes. I didn't really know Alan very well. He was a new client, and I sensed there was a lot more to him. He lived locally and knew the area well, so there was no reason for him to be late, I suppose. I bumped into him at the local shops one day, so he must have known his way around very well.'

'Bumped into him?' Peters asked.

'Yes, I was getting some lunch, and we sort of ran into each other. We just said hello, and that was that.' I noticed the detectives exchange glances like this was significant information, and instantly regretted having said it.

'A lot of our clients are local,' I added. 'That's just the way it works out. People look for services in their own area.'

'Of course, Nicole,' the detective said brusquely, but I wasn't reassured by his tone.

'Would you say you had a good counselling relationship with Alan?' Byrne asked.

'Yes, but even when the counselling relationship is good, I always keep it very professional.'

'But maybe all your clients wouldn't see it that way.'

I didn't like the implication in what he was saying, but I could see what he was trying to get at.

'Yes, but I make sure to give no conflicting signals as much as possible.'

'We've had plenty of cases where people get obsessed with someone else,' said Byrne. 'Sometimes the victim doesn't even realise it. It can lead to unforeseen consequences. I believe you had a case like that in the past where the Gardaí had to intervene?'

'Yes, I did. But I learned a lot from that experience. I feel I know what the warning signs are, and I didn't see them with Alan.'

I left with my solicitor shortly after that.

'They have to check every angle,' Kieran said, presumably to comfort me.

'I know, but it doesn't seem very constructive policing to me. Maybe they should be putting their energies elsewhere.'

'As I say, they have to take everything into account and get the full three-sixty perspective. Perhaps you should have brought up the previous stalking incident earlier.'

'This case is different. I'm sure of that now. I wanted to keep the focus on this one, but I guess they knew anyway, so maybe you're right.'

'Don't worry. You did fine, Nicole. I know it's very difficult for you. Hopefully that'll be the end of the questioning. They just need to explore every avenue,' Kieran repeated before both of us got in our cars.

As I drove home, that last sentence stuck in my head. I had to explore every avenue too. Whoever killed Alan was still out there, and with everything that had happened to me, it was impossible not to think it was all connected. Whoever did it and for whatever reason, I strongly believed that they also had me in their sights.

The person: the stalker is the killer. It made sense. What didn't make sense was why. Trying to piece everything together, I was left with no clear picture. First I was targeted; then one of my clients was killed. What was the connection between Alan and me?

I decided that the best starting point was my client. There seemed to be some correlation between the weird events and the beginning of my sessions with Alan. My initial fear that it was Gary Mulligan had faded. This felt connected to someone else. It didn't seem like an obsession, in the way Gary's fixation had turned out to be. There was more malice directed at me this time.

Even though I wasn't at work, I had access to the client database via my home laptop. When I got home, I searched Alan's profile. His background was familiar to me by now, but what I felt was missing was the detail in his background. He must have had counselling before. Maybe I could find whoever had seen him and see if they could provide some insight.

Looking through the list of care homes he had been in, I started making phone calls. The people were, of course, concerned about releasing confidential information on their clients, but I was able to pull the professional card and say it was a necessary part of a follow-up on a critical incident that had happened in my own counselling practice.

I had to put my requests in writing. That was no problem. The only issue with that was it would delay the process, and I was in a hurry. If there was valuable information to be found that would provide some clues as to Alan's past, then I wanted to have it now. I was pretty sure the Gardaí would be following similar lines of enquiry, but I felt my need to know was greater. It was a question of survival for me. Whoever killed Alan might have me in their sights now.

Pablo called over later. I was glad to see him, but the news about his brother being in town was still on my mind. It troubled me that he would keep something so important from me, and in the state of mind I was in, I didn't want any more secrets to contend with. I had to talk to him about it, find out if maybe there was more to the story that I didn't already know. When I told him I knew, he folded his arms and shook his head.

'I thought Daniel might tell you. He told me he wouldn't, and I wish he didn't, but now you know.'

'How could you keep something like that from me?'

'It was for everyone's sake. He is in real danger, and the fewer people who know, the better.'

'But what if that puts me and people close to me in danger? Aren't we entitled to know?'

'Some things you're better off not knowing. That's what I believe.'

'Is there anything more I should know? Anything else you're holding back? How can I trust you now?'

'You can trust me. The Pablo you see is the real Pablo, but I have to look after my family.'

I shook my head. 'I don't know what to believe any more.'

He held me, and we stayed like that, embraced on the couch. When we parted, I wasn't sure who or what I was dealing with.

The next morning I went into work for a couple of hours. It had been a few days since Alan's murder, and I wanted to start getting back to a semblance of normality. I wasn't going to see any clients, but I wanted to spend a little time there and go through my client files, just try to get back into some sort of rhythm.

Dorothy called in to me shortly after I arrived. I had just opened my filing cabinet and put some files on my table.

She looked sceptically at the pile.

'Nicole, I had recommended you take a good long break from work. Do you really think you're in a fit state to start going through client files?'

'I have to start back sometime. I can't just stay at home thinking all the time. It's not good. I feel scared at home, and when I think of coming back into work, that makes me scared too. There's no safe place anymore, so I want to at least try to make work a safe place.'

Even as I said that, I thought of my walking in that morning, past the space where Alan had collapsed on top of me and breathed for the last time. I had been momentarily paralysed at that spot in the hall, and my instinct had been to turn and run back to my car and get the hell out of there. But I couldn't let that happen. This was my life. I had to reclaim it. I had forced myself to walk slowly, stiffly down the hall and into my office.

'There's still a lot of police attention on this place,' said Dorothy. 'What if you run into them? What if you are seen by someone from the media? They're still around too, and I'm sure they'd love to interview you. In the state you're in, that wouldn't be a good idea, Nicole. You're so vulnerable you could say anything. Think of the other counsellors here. Think of the business.'

That's always her bottom line, I thought, *the business*. Well, I had my own life to think about, and I was determined to do anything to get it back on track.

'I'm aware of that, and I will be extremely careful and mindful about what I say, so don't worry. Alan was a client. But I also want to see what I can do to help clear up the mystery. Someone killed a client of ours, and that someone is still at large. I am looking through Alan's past to see if there's any useful information I can dig up that may help the police enquiry.'

I saw Dorothy frown heavily and shake her head. 'That is police work, Nicole, not for someone who is extremely traumatised.'

'I know it is, but if I can help, I will. I know a lot about his background – in the care homes, I mean – and I might have knowledge and access that the Gardaí don't have, so I feel obligated to use that.'

'You need to be very careful, Nicole. You are in danger of getting way out of your depth, and that, as we know from our work, can be very dangerous to someone who is traumatised.'

With that said, Dorothy walked out and left me with my files. I took a deep breath and started to sift through them.

30

DANIEL

Ben was still refusing to go to school. Pamela was threatening to stay with her parents for a while. She was falling behind with her study. Ben was apparently a constant distraction for her. I was caught between a rock and a hard place. I felt sorry for Ben, but his stubborn refusal to go was threatening to break the household up.

So I made an executive decision.

'You're going to school tomorrow, and that's final,' I said.

He was in his bedroom, a place where he had been spending increasing amounts of time. He refused to engage with Pamela at all. I was becoming seriously worried about his state of mind. Ben was a kid who had a small group of friends. He wasn't the most outgoing, so any tendency to increase his isolation wasn't good.

'You can't make me,' he said defiantly.

'You have to go. If not, the school will be after us. You can only miss so many days before they start calling to the house and asking what you are doing.' It was the educational and welfare board that did that, but I wasn't going to get into details. I hoped the thought of his school principal knocking on the door would be enough.

'They can't make me either. I want to stay with my mum not that woman out there.' He pointed in the general direction of the living room.

'I understand, Ben, I really do, and it's all going to be okay again very soon, but we have to wait until it is, okay.'

'Why does nobody tell me what's going on? Is it the person who lost their money at the zoo? Is it something to do with that?'

'No... well, maybe that was part of it, but there are a lot of things even I don't understand, so until we figure out what's happening, it's best you stay here. But you need to go to school. Once you see your friends again, you'll realise it was the right thing to do.'

I left then before he could say anything else. I could tell he would resist me all the way to the school gate, but he was going, and that was that.

'Maybe we should let him spend a little time during the day, after school, with Nicole. That might help,' I said to Pamela when I got outside.

'Yes, if she's not working. I can't have him under my feet all the time.'

I put a finger to my lips to indicate she should be careful what she said. She shook her head and went off to our bedroom.

I was going to have to speed up my investigation in any way I could. If part of that was keeping an eye on Nicole and her house, then so be it. I resolved to spend time the next evening watching who was coming and going, or to at least gauge what state of mind Nicole was in. There was a slim chance that I would see whoever it was she claimed had been following her. Could it be the same person who had killed her client? That was a scary thought, but one we had to confront.

I texted Pamela to say I would be late home, then switched my phone off. I knew she wouldn't be happy being stuck with Ben, but I felt this had to be done.

Parking my car at a row of shops about two hundred yards from the house, I walked stealthily towards the end of the road, checking and seeing nobody around. Then I found cover behind a small clump of trees that were at the entrance to the estate but gave me a clear view of Nicole's house. The evening light was fading, and car headlights swiped the trees as they passed.

Nothing happened till after 8pm when I saw Pablo drive into the estate, park his car and go into the house. That was expected. He finished work then. Given the time, he mustn't have seen his brother.

Another hour passed without anything of note happening, but then sometime after 9pm, I saw another person enter the estate. They moved to the side of the road that I was on and positioned themselves just outside a different clump of trees. I had to hold my breath and stay completely silent, afraid that I might cough or step on a twig and give away my position.

Looking closely at the male, I recognised him instantly. It was Pablo's brother.

He stood there for some time, just staring across at the house, before leaving as quietly as he had arrived.

As I watched him leave the estate, I was tempted to follow him, but then I thought he might turn back and see me coming out of the trees, so I stayed where I was for a few minutes more before I left and checked the streets outside. He had disappeared. So what was he doing there?

I hurried back to the shop car park, collected my car and

drove home. On the way I had that same nagging question running through my mind. What had he been doing there? He was obviously watching the house, but then he didn't stay long. Had he something planned and was just checking the area out?

It all seemed sinister to me.

I spoke to Pamela about it when I got home. I had to run it by someone. It had me really worried.

'Well, I told you there was something dodgy going on there. How could you trust someone who hides their identity like that?'

'I know why Pablo hid his identity, and I kind of understand that, but why would the brother be skulking around the house? That has me really worried.'

'So you should be, or should I say, *we* should be. It's something that affects both of us. We want the situation here to improve, don't we?' She nodded towards Ben's bedroom, where he was asleep.

'Well, my primary concern is Nicole's safety. Does she know what she's got herself into? I don't trust her judgement at the moment. The manner in which her client was killed has me deeply worried. Who would do a thing like that in broad daylight, and why would they choose her place of work to do it?'

'Do you think she knew anything about it?'

'No, of course not, it's just the timing and the place are so strange. There's something really off about it. The scene with Pablo and his brother... it's just not right.'

'You're telling *me* it's just not right,' Pamela scoffed. 'I think things might be getting a whole lot worse before they get better.'

Those words were repeating in my head as I got ready for bed. I was going to have to keep a better eye on Nicole. I needed a chance to talk to her as well. It was important that she knew about the brother being outside the house.

Did Pablo know? What part was he playing, and what plans did he have for Nicole?

31

NICOLE

The time off from work was doing me no good. My mind was filled with endless speculation as to what was happening. I played the scene with Alan over and over in my head. Pablo was around as much as he could be to give support, and I appreciated that. Maybe where he had come from gave him an understanding of the trauma I was going through. He was being sensitive, not asking too many questions, giving me space when I needed it. Doing the cooking, shopping, stuff that I normally did on autopilot but lately had become a big deal for me. Going to the shops caused cold anxiety to ripple through me. The world outside was filled with threat.

I decided I needed to go back to work properly, to start seeing clients again. I couldn't just leave them hanging. Thinking of what happened to Alan made me want to reach out to each one of them, to reassure them, to give them a safe space to offload their troubles before those troubles reached boiling point.

I had emailed Dorothy the night before. She would get

the email in the morning, I hoped, and by that time, I would already be in work.

As I scrolled through my emails, I spotted one from one of the care homes I had written to regarding Alan. That made my heart skip a beat. Reading it carefully, I saw that they were willing to divulge some information from Alan's background. They would let me know what services he had accessed.

I was to call in to them in two days' time, and they would release the files in person.

Brilliant, I thought, *that will at least give me some concrete information to work off. I'll be able to get a complete picture of his background. I can then contact whoever worked with him and see what they are willing to tell me.*

Armed with that news about Alan, I felt I was getting somewhere. I knew, of course, from my own work, that having a sense of agency in dealing with a crisis is always a help.

That put a bit of a spring in my step as I went into work the next morning.

I knew though that Dorothy wouldn't approve of me coming back, and I was right. She was straight down to my office before I had even seen my first client. She came into my office and closed the door behind her. It was strange, but I felt a little trapped when she did that.

Maybe I'm in an even worse state than I realise, I thought.

'Nicole,' she said gravely, 'this is not what I had recommended for you or for our counselling service. You are not in a fit state to start working with clients.'

'I understand where you're coming from, but I have a duty of care to my clients, and I have left them for long enough. Some, as you know, are very vulnerable, and they can't be left in limbo. I need to see them.'

'There are other counsellors here. We can spread the workload around.' Dorothy was staring at me, like she was trying to rattle me, but I wasn't going to give in to her pressure.

'It's the relationship between client and counsellor that is most important,' I said, 'and I have built a relationship with these clients. It might reverse a lot of the good work I have done to suddenly change their counsellor.'

Dorothy's glare softened slightly. 'You've always been conscientious with your clients, but given your past trauma and now this awful incident, you must realise that the conscientious thing to do is to take a good long break.'

'I did consider that, but it weighed too heavily on me to leave my clients in limbo. I have been working on myself and been proactive in my research into Alan's background, to try to give myself some agency. I actually made some progress in that regard. One of the care homes is willing to release files on the services Alan accessed.'

Her look became stern again. 'That is police work. You shouldn't be involved in anything like that.'

'I have to do something. You know yourself how important it is to be proactive. I'm going to see them tomorrow afternoon when they'll release the information on Alan. I see no harm in finding out what they have. It's been troubling me for a while that I didn't know that much about Alan's background. Maybe I should have tried to find out more earlier on, and that might have helped me understand exactly where he was coming from.'

'Nicole, you are losing perspective here. That's what the problem is. Of course do something that will help you, but you should in no way get involved in a police investigation.'

I tried to make her see sense. 'But this is information that I may be able to help the investigation with.'

'You need to think very carefully about what you're doing. As I said, you are not in a fit state of mind to be doing anything like that. Looking after yourself, Nicole – that's what you should be doing, not going on wild goose chases like some would-be detective. Get a grip.'

Dorothy turned and stormed out of the room.

I was left confused by her extreme reaction. Was I really losing perspective that much? I didn't think so. Our clients could sometimes be slow in revealing everything about themselves. Alan was proof of that. He'd waited for just the right time to tell me what was troubling him most. Except he never got that chance.

Now it was up to me to set that right in any way I could.

32

DANIEL

I had decided that I needed to talk to Nicole and fast. I texted her with that message, but she said she had gone back to work. That made me even more anxious to speak to her. I decided I would go to her place of work at lunchtime and wait for the right opportunity. If I texted her or called her again, she might ignore me. This was urgent.

What were Pablo and his brother up to? They obviously knew Nicole was in a very vulnerable state of mind after the killing of her client. Were they preparing to take advantage of that? Were they in any way involved in the killing and, if so, for what reason?

I had a restless morning in the shop thinking all this through. I was agitated, had a constant fear that my phone was going to light up any minute, and it would be more bad news. I had managed to get Ben into school that morning, which was a load off my mind. I had threatened him again with a home visit from his principal, and that seemed to work. I figured his behaviour was to do with everything that was going on. He was feeling insecure and acting out. School refusal was just a symptom of his insecurity. I reassured myself that everything would return to normal once we got to the bottom of what was going on, but somewhere in the back of my mind remained the concern that if Nicole was under threat, Ben could well be under threat too.

I had told Ben to wait inside the school gates until Pamela came to collect him today and not to move, to make sure that he was in sight of whatever teacher was on duty.

Just before lunch, I closed up the shop and headed for my car. The plan was to go to Nicole's work, wait for her to come out and go on lunch, and then seize the chance to talk to her. I knew from when we were married that she liked to take a stroll in a nearby park and have her lunch on a park bench that was slightly out of the way. That struck me as the perfect place for us to have a quiet chat.

I would wait near the park entrance and take the opportunity when she came along.

33

NICOLE

About mid-morning I got a call from Dorothy on our internal phone system. She obviously hadn't cooled down.

'I've been thinking about what you said and what you're up to now, playing private eye with Alan's past. It worries me, Nicole. I have our reputation to consider. That's what counselling is all about, don't you think? If word gets out that we are not trustworthy, that we go behind people's backs, then that's not going to do us any good, is it?'

'I'm not going behind anyone's back.' I was getting angry with her now. She was overstepping the mark. 'I'm doing what I can to help bring this whole thing to some sort of resolution. I am entitled to do that, and you shouldn't infer that my actions are underhand.'

Dorothy said nothing for a few seconds before speaking again. 'Nicole, I think it's time we had a real chat. I've tried to be sensitive after all you've been through, but your rash behaviour is starting to concern me. We need to have a proper talk at lunchtime. Just you and me.'

'Fine by me. I usually go to the park at lunchtime if the

weather's nice like today. I'll be doing that. If you want to come with me, that's fine.' I wasn't going to apologise for the way I felt. She wasn't treating me fairly, and she needed to realise that. If she wanted to talk, then we'd do it on my terms.

I popped out to the shop to get a sandwich and returned it to my office. Sure enough, Dorothy appeared in the hall, wearing a long coat, a wooly hat pulled low over her forehead and a bag slung over her shoulder.

She certainly isn't taking any chances with the weather, I thought.

'Okay, let's go,' she said brusquely. 'Where is it in the park you usually go?'

I described my quiet little corner in among the trees.

'I see,' she replied matter-of-factly.

We walked in silence to the park and turned in through the big wrought-iron gates.

We were only a few metres in when Dorothy stopped. 'You go on,' she said. 'I'll catch up with you. I see someone I know.'

She started walking towards a middle-aged woman with a dog, and I saw her speaking to her. I kept going until I reached the bench in among the trees. Dorothy caught up with me shortly after and sat beside me.

I took my sandwich from its paper wrapping and began to eat it. It was a cheese salad sandwich on brown bread – unremarkable – but I noticed Dorothy was staring at it. She lifted her gaze then to look at me. Her eyes, not the warmest to begin with, were even more cold and distant.

'Now, we were to have a talk, weren't we,' she said slowly.

'That's right, but I'm not changing my mind. I should say that from the outset. I need to act, to do something.'

'Of course you do,' she said mechanically. 'There's something I need to tell you too, though.'

'Oh, what's that?' I was prepared for an argument. She didn't come up here to exchange pleasantries, of that I was sure.

'The thing is, Nicole...' She stopped speaking and started fishing in her bag. She leaned in closer to me and spoke in a quiet, conspiratorial tone. 'We all have our secrets. Alan was my secret, and you are getting too close to finding out the truth.'

I looked down to see that she had pulled a huge knife from her bag, a kitchen knife with a long, pointed blade.

I couldn't believe what I was seeing, but at the same time my instincts kicked in.

'We should talk about this, Dorothy,' I said hurriedly, trying to buy time as I edged away from her on the bench. She drew the knife arm back, and that's when I tried to leap up, but she was ready. She grabbed my arm and, with a strength that shocked me, started to pull me towards her and the knife.

'There's nothing to talk about,' she hissed. 'That woman with the dog will be my witness. You came up here alone and were attacked.'

'You're crazy,' I said, desperately looking around to see if there was anyone coming. Suddenly, I heard footsteps rushing towards us, and out of the corner of my eye, I could see the blur of someone rushing Dorothy.

'Stop! What are you doing?' I recognised the voice. It was Daniel.

Dorothy turned just as he reached us, and lunged at him with the knife. He grabbed the blade, and straight away I saw bloody streams run through his fingers.

'Stop, Daniel, she's crazy!' I screamed. 'Help, somebody help!'

But Dorothy had pulled the knife back out of Daniel's hand, and she lunged again.

This time I saw the top of the blade disappear into the folds of Daniel's shirt. He froze and looked down. Blood seeped through the material.

The knife hung for a few seconds before falling with a metallic clatter to the ground. Daniel staggered towards the bench, holding his bloodied shirt against his stomach. I jumped up to help him, and at the same time, Dorothy started to run down the path. I wasn't letting her get away, so I helped Daniel onto the bench, then dashed after her.

Dorothy had her bag in her hands, and the straps were long and loose. They got caught up in her legs, causing her to stumble. With a power and a speed I didn't know I possessed, I gained on her and jumped on her back, pushing her down to the ground. As she hit the ground, I heard her head thump off it. She groaned, and her whole body went limp. I checked her face, but she was out cold. Then I checked her pulse. Strong.

I tied the straps of her bag tight around her legs and left her where she had fallen. Rushing back over to Daniel, I laid him down gently on the bench. His face was pale, and his eyes looked distant, but he managed a small smile.

I grabbed my phone and called emergency services: ambulance and police.

The rest of the scene went by in a blur. I heard sirens, saw men and women in uniforms, recounted what had happened to the police. The two detectives who had spoken to me about Alan turned up and took notes. Dorothy was taken into custody. Daniel went off in an ambulance.

I called Pablo. He came out immediately, and the two of us headed straight for the hospital. Pablo drove. On the way, I explained as best I could what had happened. He kept shaking his head and saying, 'Oh my God. My God, I don't believe it.'

We waited in the area outside surgery until Daniel was

wheeled out. He was fast asleep but stable. That was what the doctor told us.

'He's going to be okay,' the doctor added, and they were the best words I had ever heard. 'He should wake in an hour or so. He'll be very groggy though.'

'That's okay,' I said. 'I'll wait. I need to be here.'

Pablo and I headed to a café in the hospital. While we were waiting, I called Pamela.

'There's been a bit of an incident. Daniel got hurt, but he's going to be okay.'

Pamela gasped. 'Hurt how?'

'He was stabbed, but the wound isn't serious. I've just spoken with the doctor. Daniel is out of surgery already.'

'What do you mean stabbed? What happened?' Her voice was high with anxiety.

'I can't give you all the details. It happened near my work. Daniel was trying to protect me.'

'Protect you, from who?'

'I can't tell you that much now, but I'll text you the name of the hospital and the ward so you can see him later this evening.'

'Oh my God. I don't believe this. And I have so much work to do.'

'I'll be over to pick Ben up this evening,' I told her. 'He needs to be with me now. Please don't tell him anything. I don't want to scare him. I'll figure out what to tell him later.'

'You're coming over for him?' Her voice trailed off, like she was trying to figure out how to respond. I hung up on her, so she didn't get a chance to finish her thought.

34

DANIEL

I woke in the middle of the night in a private room, hooked up to machines that beeped, clicked and whirred gently. It took me a couple of minutes to figure out where I was and to slowly piece together the events of the day.

I had waited near the entrance to the park and had seen Nicole approaching. She was with another woman though, so I thought I'd missed the opportunity to talk to her. The other woman had branched off then and started talking to someone, so I'd decided I would go after Nicole. As I started walking, the other woman turned suddenly and started walking in the same direction, but in front of me. I was about to turn back, but something bothered me about her dark, heavy clothing on what was quite a nice spring day. I continued on after her, at a distance. Memories of the person at the zoo stayed with me, and her outfit reminded me of Ben's description of the person.

It gave me a queasy feeling in my stomach as I walked.

When I turned at the top of a path, I saw both Nicole and the other woman sitting on a park bench. The woman was on

Nicole's right, so she was facing me. She was rooting in her bag for something. Then I saw a flash of light as she pulled out what looked like a long knife.

I started to run. My thoughts went into a complete blur as I closed in on them. My only thought was to get the knife from her, but the woman turned as I approached, and the knife was suddenly pointed in my direction. I grabbed at it and felt a sharp pain as it sliced across my hands. Instinctively I pulled away, but the woman lunged at me, and I felt the blade slice through my shirt and into my stomach.

That made me freeze on the spot. As I stood there, I heard the knife fall heavily onto the ground.

My hands were suddenly warm and sticky with blood. I felt faint, and my eyes were blurring, but I saw the woman jump from the bench and run past me. Nicole helped me onto the bench, then went after her. Everything after that was a blur.

I remembered a paramedic with his face close to mine, trying to talk to me, but I'd been too weak to answer.

As I lay in the hospital bed, all I knew was I had been stabbed by the woman who was with Nicole. She had wanted to kill Nicole, that much was clear. She was probably the person behind all the strange stuff that had been happening. The long coat, the hat pulled down over her head and the dark clothing was a clue. She'd looked like the person described at the zoo and the person who Nicole had said had tried to push her car into traffic.

A nurse came into the room and checked the various machines I was hooked up to. She was young, fast and efficient, and made sure everything was okay. She looked at me as she worked and smiled, pleased to see I was awake.

'Well, how are we feeling?' she asked in a warm, country accent.

'Getting used to all of this,' I replied and nodded at the machines I was plugged into.

She laughed. 'Hopefully you won't have to get too used to it. Doctor will be along shortly. You have a visitor downstairs – your ex, Nicole – but we want the doctor to see you first. He'll let you know how you're getting on. Do you need anything?'

I was going to say no, but then it occurred to me there was something I needed very badly. 'Did you see my phone, by any chance?'

'Yes, here we go.' She picked it up from my bedside locker and placed it in my hands.

'Thanks. That's great,' I said and tried to smile, but every movement hurt, and even holding the phone was a real effort.

She left then, and I started the laborious and painful process of opening my phone to check the messages. Just as I thought, there was a slew of messages from Nicole, all hoping I was okay, thanking me for being there, saying that she would be up to me as soon as they let her. She said it was her boss at work, Dorothy, who had stabbed me, and she believed Dorothy had also killed Alan. Dorothy was under guard in hospital. The police were waiting to question her.

If that was true, it left the huge, unanswered question of why. If she had killed Alan, then it had probably been her who'd been harassing Nicole all along, with the intent to kill her. It was almost impossible to comprehend, that someone who was in such a position of authority would do such things. But it looked like she had. She had also tried to kill me.

I saw some texts from Pamela as well, expressing shock at what had happened and wanting to see me as soon as possible. She was looking after Ben so couldn't come straight away. I didn't have the energy or dexterity to text anyone back. Once I had read through the messages, I just let the phone drop onto my stomach. I would leave it there until the nurse or doctor came in.

I think I slept for a while because when I opened my eyes next, I saw a small team of people standing around my bed. They were all looking intently at me. I felt like a specimen or some interesting new creature that had been discovered. One guy who had a white coat over a grey suit spoke when he saw me looking at them.

'Ah, Daniel, you're back with us. I'm Dr McNamara, and this is my team.' He gestured to the mix of people standing around.

'You had quite a nasty wound there, Daniel, but we've stitched you up. We've checked you out pretty thoroughly, and the good news is there was no organ damage. It's really just a question of keeping a close eye on the injury as it heals. So we'll be keeping you with us for a few days yet.'

'Oh, right,' I replied coolly. It was good news about the wound, but my mind suddenly went to the empty shop. It couldn't just stay closed. The doctor looked a bit taken aback by my reaction, but he relaxed again quickly.

'It's natural you're going to feel in shock after what happened, so we need to take good care of you. I'll be in to see you every day, and don't worry, we'll let you go as soon as we can.'

They headed out, and I was left to stare out the window. I supposed I should have been grateful that it wasn't a whole lot worse, but I felt a surge of mixed emotions flow through me: anger at what we had been put through; relief that it looked like the nightmare might now be over; shock that Nicole's boss would do something like that.

Then Nicole appeared in the doorway, with a newspaper and a box of chocolates in hand, looking in at me. I guessed she didn't know if I was awake or asleep, so I did my best to smile at her.

'You poor thing,' she said as she approached. 'You poor, poor thing. Look what's happened to you. I feel like this is all my fault. I had to come and see you. Sorry if you're not up to a visit yet.'

'It's okay,' I croaked.

'It's crazy,' Nicole said, pulling a chair close up to my bed. 'It was Dorothy all along. I'm pretty sure she was behind everything. The knife. That's how Alan was killed. It must have been her. She said I was getting too close to her secrets. Alan was her secret.'

'What does that all mean?'

'I don't know. I expect we'll find out pretty soon though once the police have talked to her. I guess I'm very lucky that you were there. You were so brave. Why were you there though? That's been puzzling me.'

'I had to talk to you, in person, about everything that was going on. I saw you go into the park, and I followed you.'

'Well, thank God you did. I don't know how I'll repay you. But one thing I thought I could do was run the shop for you while you're laid up. I'm not going to be working any time soon, not while Dorothy is locked up. If you want to give me the keys, I'll look after it from tomorrow.'

I smiled with relief. 'They're in my pocket.'

She fished the keys from my trouser pocket, gave me a gentle kiss and left. I was exhausted after even that short interaction and fell into a deep sleep as soon as she was gone, waking every now and then to try to figure out where I was before dropping back to sleep.

Pamela dropped in later that evening. She looked a little harried as she came in, but she came straight over to the bed to kiss me.

'Nicole told me what happened. I'm sorry I couldn't come sooner, but I was looking after Ben. I didn't want him to know what happened. This is crazy. Who would do a thing like that?'

'It's a long story,' I said. 'I'm not up to talking much yet.'

She fussed around my bed as if unsure what to do or say next.

'I had flowers for you, but they wouldn't let me bring them in.'

'Oh, yes. They don't let people bring flowers in any more. Allergies.'

She wrinkled her nose. 'That's kind of stupid. What else are you supposed to bring people in hospital?'

I shrugged my shoulders and winced with the pain. It was so easy to forget not to do normal things like that, but the sharp jab of pain from my abdomen was a quick reminder.

'How are you anyway?' She rubbed my shoulder.

'I've been better, but they say I'll be okay. I'll be out in a few days. Nicole is going to look after the shop while I'm out of action.'

'That's good of her,' Pamela said with uncertainty. 'I'm kind of busy with study and all that; otherwise I'd love to help.'

'Of course.'

'By the way, Nicole came straight over this evening and took Ben without so much as a thank you or any discussion. I think it's a bit much, to be honest, after all the help that we gave, or rather, and I don't mean to sound selfish, but I gave. It really got in the way of my work and my study. Nicole obviously doesn't see that. And Ben, well, he just thinks about himself, I suppose.'

That last remark made me suddenly angry. I was lying, badly wounded in a hospital bed, and Pamela was in to gripe about different aspects of her life she wasn't happy about, and she was being very unkind about Ben. I looked at her and had a searing moment of self-awareness, when I realised I no longer loved Pamela. She looked at me, and I saw uncertainty cloud her expression.

'Pamela,' I said slowly, 'you know these recent times have been pretty difficult to say the least, and in difficult times, sometimes we see a different side to people. I'm sorry, but I think it's best if we call it a day. If we're honest about it, maybe we should have called it a day a while back.'

Pamela jerked back a few feet on the bed and stared at me, like she was checking it was really me who was speaking.

'What? Is that really what you want?'

'Yes, it is. I'm sorry, but it is. I'm sure of it, and I think it's best for you too. It just hasn't been working very well this past while.'

She got angry. 'Oh, nice. That's really nice, that is. I come in to comfort you and say nothing about how stupid you were to put yourself in danger like that. Well, maybe you're right. Maybe it is time we went our separate ways.'

She stood up dramatically and stalked to the door, then whirled around. 'Oh, and thanks very much for nothing. I'm not surprised that stupid bitch broke up with you.'

I was left dazed by her words. What I had said was a knee-jerk reaction. It had just come out. Pamela was behaving so selfishly, had behaved so selfishly since the beginning of the difficulties for Nicole. Now with her reaction, I felt she had just shown her true colours.

Maybe saying what I did was the best thing. I felt a weight lifted from my shoulders. It was only then that I realised I had been carrying Pamela's anger as well as everything else.

Maybe this was a chance to make a fresh start.

35

NICOLE

The weeks passed by. Daniel got out of hospital and was expected to make a full recovery. Dorothy was still in custody, and the case against her seemed to drag on. I guessed they were just being cautious and making sure the case was watertight. I was interviewed a couple more times; details of the events had to be gone back over. That was okay by me. I wanted to put the whole thing behind me as soon as possible.

The counselling practice had fallen apart. Understandably, none of the clients wanted to return, and there was no interest from anyone to buy the business. I felt terrible for the clients, so I went through my database and referred each one on to other counselling practices.

I had my own troubles. The money I was earning in Daniel's shop was just about keeping the wolf from the door. I took minimum wage because I knew he needed every penny he could get. Even more so now that he had missed so much time in the shop. He would be back in soon enough, and then I was going to be officially unemployed.

Then a beacon of hope appeared.

A friend of mine who worked in education told me about a couple of special-needs assistant vacancies that had come up in her school. They were finding it hard to fill the places. She told me I had so much experience working with a broad range of client needs that I would be perfect.

I interviewed, and despite the fact I told them I was involved in a long court case, I got the job. I would be working with children under the age of twelve with additional needs, and I would start as soon as I was Garda vetted. That process took a couple of weeks, and I had to borrow a little money from the credit union to get by, but it was a fresh start – albeit it on a lower wage than I was used to at the practice.

However, it meant a break from counselling while I recovered from my ordeal. There was no way I was fit to counsel anyone.

Ben was excited by my new job, even though it wasn't at his school.

'So you'll be like Sophie in our school?' She was the special needs assistant for his class group.

'I suppose so. Do you think I'll be any good?'

'You're older than Sophie, Mam, but you're kind too, so you'll be good.'

'Well, thank you for the vote of confidence, young man.'

'You're welcome, Mam. I'm glad I'm back here and not with Pamela.'

Daniel had told me that he and Pamela had split up, so Ben wouldn't be able to go there until he had recovered enough to look after him. He was out of hospital and able to get around, but he was still in pain. I told him I'd look after Ben until he was fully back on his feet.

Then I received word from the Gardaí. A court date had been set, and the book of evidence had been completed. They were able to fill me in on what the prosecution had decided on. Enough evidence had been gathered to charge her with the murder of Alan and assault with a deadly weapon on Daniel.

'We have a motive for why she killed Alan,' Detective Byrne told me. 'When he was in the care home a few years ago – he would have been sixteen at the time – Dorothy was his counsellor, and it appears they had a sexual relationship. He was underage at the time, so if anyone found out, she would have been liable for criminal charges. When she saw him come into your counselling service, she panicked. She started stalking you, trying to make it look like you were crazy and hoping to get you off his case. When that didn't work, she started to get more desperate. She admitted to trying to push your car into traffic. She was using cars from a shared car scheme so it wouldn't be obvious it was her car. She had it all worked out. Unfortunately it didn't work, so she killed Alan. Then you started looking into his past, the care home end in particular, so she had to get rid of you.'

'Nice,' I said. 'My own boss, who would have thought?'

'Well, she is where she belongs now, and my guess is she won't be getting out for quite a long time.'

'Good is all I can say to that. I knew she wasn't the warmest of people, but who would have thought she was that bad?'

'She had a lot to cover up, and she was willing to do anything to keep it hidden.'

'Yeah, the business was everything to her. I would have thought human life was too, given her profession, but apparently not.'

The court case took place some weeks later, and Dorothy tried to put in a plea of manslaughter. She admitted to killing Alan but said it wasn't premeditated. The judge didn't buy it, and she got handed a life sentence. Both Daniel and I had to appear as witnesses, but at least it was for one session only.

On the day I was there, Dorothy looked pale, frail and drawn, a shadow of her former fiery, feisty self.

I wondered, as I observed her, if it was partly an act to sway the judge's opinion. It didn't work, and I was glad. Normal life could slowly start resuming.

Pablo was around a lot. He was supportive to both me and Daniel, giving Daniel breaks at the shop when he needed. Daniel really appreciated it, but he told me something about Pablo that he hadn't said before. He had seen Pablo's brother outside my house one night, like he was watching the house. That worried me, so I brought it up with Pablo one evening.

'I have something I wanted to ask you.'

'Yes, anything, my love.'

'Okay, this is kind of hard to say, but Daniel was worried about me, so he was keeping an eye on the house. He saw your brother hide in the estate one night, like he was watching the house.'

Pablo smiled and shook his head. 'I'm sorry about that. It was a time when we were really stressed about everything, and my brother's phone was broken. He needed to contact me badly. I should never have told him where you live, but I worried a lot about him, and if he really needed me, what would he do?'

'That's not cool, Pablo. You know that. I don't want any attention drawn to my house, not while there are people who are after your brother.'

'I know. I am really sorry. I shouldn't have, but let me tell you some news. My brother is gone now. He won't be back. He has a place in Spain with his friend and a new identity. I will go and visit him sometime but not for a while. He needs to lie really low. There will be no more secrets. I promise you that. You are the most important thing in my life. And what's more, I got you this.'

He reached into his pocket and pulled out a small velvet-covered case, which he opened to reveal a beautiful, custom-made gold ring with a sparkling, green amethyst stone in the middle.

'I see this in Daniel's shop, and I have to get it. You can think about it. I don't want to put no pressure on you. I gave you a ring before, but this time I want the ring to be an engagement ring.'

He smiled, and I saw the honesty in his deep, brown eyes. I didn't have to think too long.

I started my job as a special needs assistant a couple of weeks later. It was so strange to be in the middle of such energetic kids, but it was a really refreshing change. I would finish my day at the same time as Ben, and we were able to spend some lovely afternoons together.

I noticed that I was still quite nervous though, checking doors two or three times at night, listening out for any unusual sounds. I knew the trauma of what had happened was still very much with me, so I took the extra step of going back to counselling. It felt strange being back in a therapist's room, this time on the other side of the table, but it was something I needed to do for Ben, for Pablo, for the kids I was working with and for myself.

Daniel eventually made a full recovery. I helped him out every now and then in the shop, covering Saturdays – anything that would give him a break and help his recovery. He and Pamela were still broken up.

'I don't know what I was thinking,' he'd say now and again, or, 'Was I thinking at all?' whenever her name came up. He seemed happier, more carefree. I sympathised with him over the split, but, personally, I was glad that Ben didn't have to spend any more time with her.

Pablo tells me his brother managed to carve a life out for himself in Spain, living quietly, staying off social media, not drawing any attention to himself. I know Pablo calls him every now and then, and that's okay. I don't need to know any more about it.

We have our routine and our quiet, peaceful lives. I am hoping that soon, with therapy, I'll be able to relax fully into that life.

ABOUT THE AUTHOR

Kevin is a Guidance Counselor by day and a psychological thriller author during his off hours. He puts an original slant on some common experiences and creates engaging stories with a personal twist. Kevin lives in Dublin, Ireland with three great kids, a frenetic Westie, Alfie, and a wife who makes him laugh, which is really all he could ask for.

Want to connect with Kevin? He'd love to hear from you via email - kevinmflynch@gmail.com

Did you enjoy *The Secret*? Please consider leaving a review on Amazon to help other readers discover the book.

ALSO BY KEVIN LYNCH

SOMEBODY OUT THERE

THE PERFECT HOME

THE SECRET

THE LAKE